AN EYE for
~~AN EYE~~ MY LOVE

AN EYE for
~~AN EYE~~ MY LOVE
I want to live

Vibhor Tikiya

Srishti
PUBLISHERS & DISTRIBUTORS

SRISHTI PUBLISHERS & DISTRIBUTORS
Registered Office: N-16, C.R. Park
New Delhi – 110 019
Corporate Office: 212A, Peacock Lane
Shahpur Jat, New Delhi – 110 049
editorial@srishtipublishers.com

First published by
Srishti Publishers & Distributors in 2017

Dedicated to my mother, and with lots of love to my beautiful nieces, Kimaya and Annika. I love you guys and I hope you always find peace and happiness. May the country that you see be much more evolved when you grow up than the one in this book.

Foreword

Justice can't always be achieved by Law

I am proud of my nation and have always been so. I remember times when to motivate myself all I had to do was hear the national anthem. It propped me up like nothing else.

But like every nation, we have our share of animals and they do their bit to ensure that the darkest sides of this country are visible for all of us to see. The Delhi gang rape was one such horrific example that made our souls tremble. It was the worst of mankind manifesting itself. Anger, pity and many more emotions come to us when we think about it and yet we aren't able to do anything. To a degree, I can vent my frustrations in print, but it won't bring her back and many others whom we have lost to this menace.

A lot of times, we look for reasons as to why would God create these animals who have little or no respect for women. But, I guess, life is what it is and there is no reason behind many random evils that happen to good people.

I remember people protesting about the incident in one of the forums that I went to and asking an eminent lawyer about the use of such protests.

"These protests are for our future generations. One generation suffers, the other protests, and the third benefits. This is a movement for change."

What about the life lost? What about this generation? What about the parents who gave birth and love to a small child who was ravaged years later by these animals?

They called her Nirbhaya – the fearless one. I didn't understand the name at first. The one thing that caught my attention in that gangrape incident was the fact that Nirbhaya wrote on a letter to her mother saying *"I want to live."* It is fearlessness that a girl who has seen the worst this society has to offer still has the strength to battle for her life. It is fearlessness that she fought for her life as long as she did after the savagery that she had been through.

This book is not her story, but takes off from her statement and is dedicated to the victims of rape across the country with a hope that a day will come that whenever such books are written, they are a distant historical account about a menace which existed once upon a time. I hope the generation after me thinks that this book is dated. I hope the generation after me has no Nirbhaya who has to go through the ordeal ours did. I hope the villain ceases to exist and every woman lives without Bhaya.

Life is a gift and no one has the right to take it from anyone else. NO ONE!

Prologue

"What is this life if it is not worth dying for something?"
—*Martin Luther King.*

"While she was in the hospital fighting for her life, she looked at me and asked for a piece of paper and a pen. I thought she wanted to tell me who did this to her, so I could fight for her. I thought she wanted me to take revenge and make that guy pay, but she didn't write that. On that piece of paper, she wrote something that will haunt me for the rest of my life."

The group stared at me, tears in all of their eyes as well. One or two even held me close and tried to calm me down.

I took out the piece of paper from my pocket and put it down in front of absolute strangers who had but just one thing in common.

The paper said: *'Dhruv, I want to live.'*

Bravado and craziness often go together and often need a motive. There has to be a reason for someone who puts everything on the line. I guess I was holding on to a thought, the essence of being in love with someone. It was a crazy idea, just the feeling of being at that place in your life.

When you wander without a purpose, you get the feeling you're drowning, and that time's running out. You hold on to that first hand you can see so that you don't sink in. That hand has to be it – the love of your life, the person you were supposed to spend the rest of your life with and all that jazz. After a while, you don't check back on that feeling. You don't give it a beta test or anything.

Now imagine the aforesaid hand snatched away from you. If that happens, the response of the man who almost drowned can be so extreme that the outcome can potentially surprise you. I was that man, the individual without direction. I was born with a golden spoon and I had no intention to make it into a diamond one. I wasn't one of those youngsters who had a drive. For me, life was a random process, the outcome of which was so heavily dependent on luck that you might as well enjoy it on the way. My life was full of travels and adventures funded by my late father's interest-generating instruments.

I was aptly named Dhruv, living the life fit for a prince. But for all the randomness that life has to offer, one would least expect me to be hit by sticks and face tear gas. When that sacrifice didn't work, I had all but one shot of the gun to offer. My life had come down to getting this right. No one except two random men knew that I was doing this and there was a good chance that, win or lose, in both situations, no one would ever bother to find out why I did what I did.

Life had taken me from being the reckless globetrotter to the fundamentalist murderer. They say it can be very weird and change each and every fundamental truth in and around you whenever the hell it desires to. It doesn't take much; a few years, months, days or even moments for you to awaken to a new reality. For the lucky ones, that reality is love. For unfortunate ones like me, the reality was loss.

I see myself and there are so many different faces. I wonder how my final judgement will be. I am a criminal who is guilty of murder. I am a lover who has been scorned. I am a hero who was never meant to be. That was not what it was supposed to be though. I was named Dhruv because of what the name stood for – a prince.

Maybe, I still am the prince, but in a different sense. Perhaps, I was meant to be '*Che*'. These are my motorcycle diaries.

I want to live

When I call out your name, no one answers.
It is your essence that I miss the most,
Your smile, the energy you carried with you,
Moments of life when I felt alive were all with you,
You took my soul with you, leaving behind a carcass,
Take me with you, don't leave me behind,
I am all alone, all alone, all alone.

I remember your call, your cry,
Your desire to continue living,
It doesn't let me sleep, doesn't let me live.
I await the day I die so I can be with you,
In your arms,
No one should go through what I did,
No one should be all alone, all alone, all alone...

Vengeance

"Will I be great, Maa? Will I be famous?"
"Pain and glory go hand in hand, son;
Glory won't come that easy though
It'll have its share of pain
And the day you overcome the pain, son
You will be truly great."

"You've got one shot," said Aryan while feeding on chips that were completely inappropriate for the situation given how tense it was. Yet he seemed unreasonably cool. Something about him was unsettling.

"Why do I have only one shot? Can you please stop having those chips. We're here to kill someone."

"I know. If you're calmer, you'll do this well, just like we trained. You can't have nerves."

He looked at me and smiled. We were in a dilapidated building, one which did not belong in the heart of the city, but was still here. There were some cracks in the walls and it was scheduled to go for redevelopment, but some minister ate up all the funds. Some egotistic, money and power-crazy man, exactly the kind we were set to kill tonight. India was full of them and I was about to get rid of one.

He looked at me, "I have a way to calm you down. What do you see?"

"I see a busy street…"

"No, no apart from your target, you have to see and imagine your motive. You have to focus for a while on why you're doing this. Close your eyes for a minute."

I closed my eyes. After a while, I opened them and looked at him.

He gave me an inquisitive look, "So?"

"I see a girl running towards her dreams. I see her parents watching her with lots of love. I see her running uninhibited and free, not giving a rat's ass to the crap around her. I see her ready to embrace love if it comes her way. I see a girl with a deep desire to live. I see a man with a gun ready to shoot any asshole who comes in her way without hesitation."

He gave me a smile. "Now you're ready."

We were in a room with nothing except a window pane which gave a clear view of the area below. It was almost as blank as my future after this. There was a good chance that I was going to be arrested and be in a jail cell which was probably going to be devoid of both light and furniture, and be worse than the enclosure we currently were in. The colours were pale, almost signifying death. The mood was very somber and the only noise was the faint one of vehicles passing by. The sound of chips was therefore resounding and quite rattling.

There was constant traffic downstairs. My stomach was in my mouth. I was shit scared. "What happens if I miss?"

"Well, his guards will get pushed in high alert and form an enclosure around him if the shot misses. There will be a granular search of everything around and we might be caught."

"Won't we be caught even if we make the shot?"

"There's a chance, but then a percentage of his bodyguards will be in shock for some moments and try to save their master. We need to exit then."

"How do we exit?"

"Have you ever done rapelling?" He then paused. "What is wrong with you? We have trained for all of this. Why are you asking so many questions?"

I stared at him. "Just answer my questions. I am looking for some reaffirmation."

He pointed towards the window at the back of the house. There was a perceived anchor in the form of a table. That's what the goddamn rope was for. We were going to go down the building with a rope tied around our stomach.

"The whole thing just feels like a nightmare."

"Look at me. It is too late to have second thoughts."

He continued munching on his chips while I stared at him. He wanted me to use that rope for jumping down that dilapidated building into a garbage disposal with a rope tied around my waist.

Aryan smiled. "You're Tom Cruise a.k.a. Mission Impossible."

"I don't know if I'll be able to do that, man."

"Well, I think we've crossed the point where we're measuring ability to perform a task. We did that while training already. Hereinafter, everything is a necessity."

I pointed the holster in his direction. "What if I kill you? I have more than one clear shot."

"You could. Except you didn't train to kill me. You are an assassin trained to shoot down one man. You're like the man in terminator – Arnold was looking to terminate just one target. You can't rest until you finish him. After that, your task will be over. I will prepare acid water for you to jump into and self-terminate."

"How can you make jokes at this time?"

"My estimate is it will be one hour before he passes by this area. We anyway need to pass our time. You look nervous. The best way to calm you down is this."

I looked at him and smiled. We were both in dull-coloured outfits that could not be spotted from afar. In fact, we gelled so much into the colours of the wall of the flat that a passerby could hardly make out if there were two figures in the house. I was at the window with my holster tucked away. We were both on the back side of the window to make sure no one realized we were there.

I was more nervous than Aryan. This was my first time in executing a person. It was difficult for me to fathom how I reached this point. However, I prevented myself from thinking at that juncture, lest my willpower fade away.

Desire for vengeance is probably the most dangerous of all emotions. It conquers everything else and consumes you if you are not able to deal with it or somehow achieve it. The Mahatma once said, "An eye for an eye makes the whole world go blind." But I don't know if that's true in today's day and age. If you do not take an eye for one taken from you, the person you spare will continue to commit offences. He will continue to violate other human beings. Justice restores balance in the world, and if the stupid legal system did not do its job, somebody had to.

It was a busy street with an important admin office where the concerned target was purported to work. He came there daily between 1-1:30 p.m. Fortunately for us, he did not classify for Z security cover. Apparently, his life was not under any perceivable threat and his office was not that important.

This building we were in was an eyesore in that area. No one bothered. The residents of the building were mainly investors eagerly waiting for redevelopment while they resided somewhere else, so there was hardly anyone living there. There was a security guard, but he hardly manned the area since there were very few visitors. We were able to enter without anyone noticing. Obviously, after the gunshot, things would be very different. The guard would be alerted and also all the people around.

That thought reminded me of a quick question. "How much time do you think we have to escape getting caught?"

"About ten minutes to rappel our way out of here and cross the gate at the opposite side."

I stared at him. "There is a good chance of us getting caught, then."

He looked at me with a blank expression on his face. "Of course. This task was always fraught with risk, man. What the hell did you train for?"

"I don't know. It just seems very different when you're actually about to execute the task."

"You have to focus. We cannot get this wrong. If people like him get shot and die, they are hardly a risk. If they survive, they don't leave the person who dared to try and take their life."

"Clearly. I have to get it right."

"Yes. Exactly the situation you trained for. There isn't much time left now. I am going to shut up from here and you are going to build on your focus. Try and get your head and soul behind it. I would tell you to remember what crap he did to you, but that would also divert your attention. Right now, you need to get this gunshot right where it was intended."

He didn't speak a word after that. There was pin drop silence in the room. There were some noises coming from below, but my mind was gradually fading them out. Mentally, I was reaching the phase that I was supposed to. I had blanked most of my thoughts out. The surroundings did not matter from here on. I was on the lookout for the target who was supposed to enter in the horizon of my vision at any moment. I had to get the shot right for his brain to explode out.

My mind got heavier. I tried to clear it of all thoughts. I had trained for this. I allowed my head to have a fleeting memory of her so that I could remind myself of why I was about to take a life. I could feel my stomach get heavier and my heart started pounding.

The exact moment of the shot also had to be well-timed. The surroundings had to be relatively stagnant for about five seconds which was the amount of time the bullet would take to travel. The shot had to hit him perfectly so that there was so possibility of resurrection.

After a while, I could hear the sound of my breath. I had indeed been trained by the perfect warrior.

A white Mercedes Benz suddenly stopped and out came the man I was meant to kill.

For a moment, everything flashed in front of my eyes. A tear rolled down my cheeks ruing everything that the man I was about to kill had done. I pressed the trigger and felt the bullet leaving my gun. This was it. My moment of glory or self-destruction was here…

Your moment of glory will come the day the desire to overcome becomes much more than the pain that comes with it.

The irrestistible
Moroccan women

"Will I see the world, Maa? Will I have wonderful experiences?"
"You will have wonderful experiences, son
People will come and go
Some will be a fleeting memory
Some will love, others will cheat
Remember them all, my dear son
For it will serve you well."

It was a roadside café which was typical of Morocco. Everything had a lazy feel about it. Apparently, Casablanca was supposed to be more vibrant but Rabat had a special feel about it. It was more 'Moroccan' than Casablanca. The Moroccan tea was brilliant. Served in a shot glass, the hot sweet concoction was literally paradise in a tea-cup. The women who served were more beautiful than actresses back home. They were literally goddesses.

The waitress walked up to me with a bill in her hand after we were done.

I looked up to her and smiled. "Yes. They don't have your name on the menu, do they?"

She was blushing and I sized her up. She had what was the perfect frame. Luscious lips, a full bosom, fair skin and features to die for. She was exactly my type.

After a pause, she replied, "Naziha."

"Hmm…so what are you doing tonight?"

"Who wants to know?"

"I know a good-looking guy who might be interested."

She quipped with a sexy look on her face, "Well you tell him my number is 04325643. He can call me up."

I gave her a sly look. I had something to do this evening. It had become difficult to find something. It had become difficult to find something different to do every day, but I got by. I guess that was because I was a hardworking man.

An old man who was watching this conversation with a lot of interest somehow had the curiosity to know more about me. I generally preferred to keep myself aloof and part of the crowd. I always figured people in this part of the world minded their own business. However, in this case, I couldn't avoid his questions.

"Where are you from?"

"India."

He frowned. Apparently, Indians were not very popular in Morocco.

"So," said the old man with a bit of dismissiveness in his voice and a slight Arabic accent, "What do you do?"

With the way he was going, I hoped Naziha was not his daughter. I replied cautiously, "I don't do anything useful. I am a globetrotter, a vagabond, if you may please."

"Who pays for your travels?"

"My late father had a lot of money. He left a lot of balance in his accounts. I made deposits out of those. Back home in India, you earn a lot of interest on these fixed deposits. I live out of that interest."

"Good-for-nothing, eh?"

I slightly raised my hat and then put it back down, "That's me."

"Did your rich father give you a name?"

"He called me Dhruv."

"What does that mean?"

I looked at him with a smile on my face. "It means 'the prince'."

He shook his head in disapproval. I was wearing a t-shirt that day which I had picked up from the market. It had a picture of a man on it with a weird beard and a rebellious look on his face. It seemed like it was me on a shirt.

"You know what you are wearing, son?"

"No."

"That's a picture of Che...Ernesto Che Guevera. He was one of the biggest revolutionaries to ever take birth. You're not inspired by him?"

"Not really. I just bought it because the colours looked good."

He looked at me as if I deserved to die. I was used to these condescending looks. I simply winked at Naziha, settled the bill and quietly got out of the cafe.

I ignored the old man while I was walking out. What the hell did I have to do with Che? I had in fact thought the man on my T-shirt was a rockstar. At least, that's what the seller had told me. I had been bloody cheated. This T-shirt was attracting attention. He had got me off my high of getting a date with Naziha.

There was a motorcycle stand outside. I walked up to the stand and asked the man there if they were on rent. He said something in French which was completely alien to me.

"English please."

"1200 dirham for a day and you have to leave your passport with me."

"I don't mind. Which bike will you give me?"

He showed me an excuse for a bike which was run down. It looked like a mean machine which would zoom on the streets of

Morocco at a blinding speed of 25-30 kmph. I would be pitted against the wind on this garage wreck.

"I am not going to pay 1200 for this."

He looked at the bike and then looked up again, "Then no bike for you."

I shook my head in disapproval and walked away from here. He immediately shouted, "600 dirham is my last offer."

I turned and in true Antonio Banderas style, lifted my hat and said, "400 and not a penny more."

He frowned and said, "Done."

It was early morning and as per my schedule, I was supposed to be on the streets by 11 a.m. Eight-nine hours of exploring the countryside and a few hours for exploring Naziha. I had a packed schedule ahead of me.

There wasn't a lot of traffic in Rabat. I guess when one is used to the streets in Bombay, traffic anywhere doesn't seem too much of a problem. I took off with a bike in my hand and the world in the offing.

Rabat has an amazing feel to it. Roadside cafes and a number of Moroccan restaurants offering traditional Moroccan cuisine, it is home to the political who's who of the country and the city is full of political offices. It was much less cosmopolitan than Casablanca, but the women here were more beautiful.

Life had been kind to me. I had no complaints with anything. I was decently well-educated and did nothing for a living. I liked my job-profile. It was to explore the world and find a bank or an ATM wherever I could. I was '*free*' in the real sense, with no boundaries, no obligations and no purpose. This kind of a life suited my personality.

There were a lot of ministerial offices in Rabat and the primary language spoken was French. It was very difficult to get directions from people if you got lost. They hardly knew any English and the little bit that they did know was quite broken. I somehow struggled and managed even after going large distances.

I was on my way to a beach just on the outskirts of the city. It was a long drive and I was almost on foot. I stopped over at a typical Morrocan restaurant. There was slight Arabic music playing and the ambience was a bit dark. There were classy vessels shaped like inverted domes for serving the typical Moroccan Tagine. I ordered a Moroccan Chicken Tagine and started to devour my food.

"Don't eat your food so fast, son."

"Don't interrupt me, Maa. I am very hungry."

There was this sadness in her eyes. A lot of the sadness could be attributed to the fact that her husband had left her and that her son was useless. He had left us a huge fortune out of guilt, but had left a void in my mother's heart and hatred in mine.

"Your bill, Monsieur."

"What?"

"Your bill."

I shook myself up a bit. I was staring through a clear glass from a classy restaurant looking at the administration buildings which were quite hazy and had zoned out for a while. It was a foggy evening and Rabat was buzzing as usual. It had all the misgivings of a big city, yet there was something about this city that was not as mechanical as the other ones I had been to. People were calmer, slower and not too obsessed about their vocation.

I got up from the restaurant and moved towards the main city for my date. I was meeting a hot brunette Moroccan beauty for dinner and sex, in that order. I didn't want to be late, lest I be replaced by some other vagabond.

I reached the prescribed meeting location just in time for my date and she showed up looking sultry and minimally dressed. We settled down for our dinner and some light conversation.

She had a heavy accent to her English. For the love of me, I couldn't figure out whether it was Arabic or French. "What is your name?"

"Dhruv."

"That's a nice name. What does it mean?"

"It means the prince."

"So which country are you from?"

"India"

"Wow. That's a very mysterious kind of place."

"Yeah. You've been in Morocco all your life?"

"Yes. So what do you do?"

"I'm a perpetual tourist."

"Do you get money for being a tourist?"

"No. I get money in other ways."

"Oh. So you have a family?"

"I used to have one. There's no one left now."

She pouted with her full, red lips. "That's so sad."

We talked about a variety of things that evening and it culminated with us in a motel, wrapped around each other with very little space between our naked, sweating bodies. We went at each other like animals and the night gradually gave way to the morning sky.

Early morning, she was watching me as I was getting out of the motel room. "So, where are you going to go? You should stay here with me."

I looked at her with a sad smile on my face. "I told you I'm a drifter, a man without purpose…unwilling to settle."

"No man is born without purpose. You just haven't found yours."

"I think some men are. Few of us are blessed to experience things without effort. Maybe that's why they named me a prince."

She smiled at me with a hint of sadness on her face. She probably expected our meeting to be a casual one-night liaison but somewhere in the back of her mind felt it could have been longer. She watched me get out of the room. I waved goodbye and took off.

People will come and go in your life. You will remember some as a fleeting memory and some will make an indelible impression…

A thousand minarets

"I hate being cheated. Why do people cheat, Maa?"
"Trust is very valuable, son.
You will be cheated on multiple times,
Love the people you learn to trust, son.
Hold them close to you,
And never lose their trust."

"This is magnificent. I have never seen something like this. You guys are lucky to live here in front of this sight," I told the local tourist guide who was showing me around.

We were standing right in front of the biggest pyramids in Cairo and it felt great. It felt as if a part of the Egyptian culture was calling out to me. The desert sun shone on the magnificent geometrical structure as it towered over us. The sun was quite harsh and our shadows were clearly visible in the sands.

"We aren't as lucky as you are, sir. You can admire this structure for half an hour, an hour at most, but after that you have to continue with normal life. That part is getting more and more difficult in Egypt. We are poor with little to eat. Our children are feeding on bread crumbs while the rich in Egypt are getting richer," replied Ahmed, my guide.

I looked at him with surprise, "But you guys have tourism, right? There is a huge influx of tourists every day to Egypt. You guys must be making tons of money."

14

"That is now an illusion, sire. The number of tourist guides outnumber the tourists, because that seems to be one of the only viable sources of income here. We have been let down by our monarch."

His eyes then swelled up. "I have small children, sire. They ate bread crumbs yesterday. Today I was lucky to get you as a client, so I will be able to feed them well."

His sad story was spoiling my high. I took out a wad of dollars in my pocket and gave some to him. I think his eyes moistened, but I hardly paid attention.

I was standing right in front of the miraculous pyramids. There was one really huge pyramid right in front of us.

I asked him, "Which pyramid is this?"

"The Pyramid of Khufu, sire. It was built for the great pharaoh Khufu. He had two very beautiful wives. He ruled Egypt for sixty-three years."

I looked at him and smiled. "Only two wives? These pharaohs were supposed to have four or five wives, no?"

He gave a coy look. "Only two, sir. He was like me."

"Oh, you have two wives too."

"Yes, I have five kids from the both of them."

"So, ten in total or five from the two."

"Five, sire. I cannot afford ten kids."

I smiled at him. "Clearly you can't even afford five. You have two wives. How do you expect to feed eight mouths."

"Allah is great, sir. He will make arrangements for my children. He sent you to me today, and will send someone for my children again, sire."

I smiled with a distinct smugness and with a hint of sarcasm in my voice told him. "Why didn't he send someone to you day before?"

With humility in his voice, he replied, "Allah is great, sir. Who are we to question his actions?"

I sighed and continued looking at the sight in front of me. You hear about it, you see it in pictures, but it's different when you're standing at striking distance. The sun was shining bright on the sand below, making our shadows large enough to cover a substantial part of the pyramid. At least, some aspect of our personas was not overly miniscule in front of the giant structures.

There wasn't much noise around, which made the setting even more perfect. I zoned out for a while.

"Mom, are you all right?"

"I don't know, Dhruv. I'm not sure if I am."

The sight of that hospital bed scared me. I was, after all, a fifteen-year-old and the one person in the whole wide world who I loved the most was dying.

"Don't leave me, Mom."

"There was so much in life that I wanted to do together with you, Dhruv. I wanted to travel the world. Go to the US, Canada, stand in front of the pyramids."

"We can still do that, Mom."

She hugged me and I somehow knew even as a fifteen-year-old that my mother was not going to make it from this illness.

"Sire, you want to go?"

I shook myself up a little bit. "Yes yes, Ahmed. Let's get out of here."

We took off from there in half an hour.

"So Ahmed, my man, any good girls for me in this city?"

"You want to marry an Egyptian woman, sire?"

"Marry? Are you crazy? I just want to have fun."

Ahmed looked at me and coyly touched his beard. "Sir, how much are you ready to spend?"

"Depends on the woman you get for me, Ahmed."

"Done, sire. I will not let you down."

I was an alcoholic, a sex-addict and a perpetual lost soul, both literally and mentally. If ever there was an advert for how *not* to lead your life, I was the purported center piece. Yet, there was no regret, fear or shame. I guess you need to be agnostic to those feelings if you want to continue down the road I was travelling.

We took off from the pyramids travelling Egypt's dusty roads. Apart from the pyramids, the rest of Egypt was like any other Indian tier one city. Slightly underdeveloped, poverty and a souvenir seller at every nook and corner – the main city wasn't far away in its mannerism from India. We went up to the Nile where I decided to take a quick dip. The water wasn't nearly as clean as I expected it to be and the banks within the city were overpopulated by concrete constructions. I took off my clothes and took a dip nevertheless, just to complete the experience.

In the evening, we took off to the hotel. Ahmed arranged the most beautiful girl I could have ever found in Cairo. He sent her up to my hotel room where I was all alone. She was the perfect Egyptian beauty. She was strikingly white, with sharp features. Most strikingly, her eyes were blue just like the Nile. She was wearing a skimpy dress with her navel and breasts partly visible. She had worn a skirt with a flowing red fabric over it.

She looked at me with a sensuous look that took me into overdrive. I took her in my arms and started kissing her body while gently taking off her clothes. I gently touched her navel and lifted her in my arms. Her lips were full and I could not take my eyes off her lovely face. I kept kissing her.

As we reached the bed, she sensuously freed herself from my grasp for just an instant and pushed me on the bed. She then backed away towards the door. I was excited as to what her next move would be.

Suddenly the door opened and two goons came into the room. I was shocked as things happened too fast for me to respond. One of them hit me on my head with a iron bar and I blacked out.

The next morning, everything I owned was gone. All my material possessions were missing. My money, clothes, shoes, accessories were all missing. They had left me high and dry.

I tried hard to remember the faces of the goons and was quite sure one of them was Ahmed.

You will be cheated on in life multiple times, which will make you appreciate the people you learn to trust even more. Don't let go of them, and more importantly, never lose their trust.

An evening in Paris

"Mom, you never met your soulmate, did you?"
"Soulmates are partners of one's soul, son.
I have one who will live much beyond me
My soul will love through his memories, son.
You are my soulmate, son.
'Coz my soul's a part of you."

"Are you my soulmate?"
"While you are mine,
You will meet yours soon.
A whiff of fresh air
She will re-define you
And purify your soul and existence."

Never trust a man's tears. His sorrow often masks a vulnerability that could very quickly cause desperation and deception. Ahmed had just fleeced me, playing both the sexual and noble aspects of my persona.

I had not bothered to file a complaint. It didn't make sense because prostitution was illegal and the genesis of my problem was indulging in the same. I would probably face a more severe penalty than the offenders.

The net worth of the valuables stolen from me in dollar terms was $2500. This wasn't that big an amount for me, but it was huge for Ahmed and his five kids…that is, if they really did exist. I guess it was charity for me in some way. That explanation provided solace, at least, in my head.

I decided to carry on with my sojourns. I had had enough of Africa; It was time to move to a richer continent. I decided to start with the romantic capital of the world, Gay Paris. Paris has a certain charm about itself. There was something very different about the city from anything I had ever seen. There is a distinct romantic feel to the entire city. It felt familiar. Leave aside touristic attractions such as the Louvre or the Eiffel, the charm of Paris was in the smaller details: the quaint cobblestone streets, prettily trimmed trees, perfectly puffed pastries, dainty tea salons and much more. It was a pleasure to just stroll down in the night. The city was buzzing, roads were clean and the bars were full of merriment.

People around me were quite fashionable. It was like walking in a fashion show. I fell in love with the city in minutes. I stopped at a bar and ordered a beer for myself. There was a beautiful girl standing alone. She looked Indian and had a distinct aura to her. She was slightly wheatish and her figure was picture perfect. There was something mystical about her. She was sitting alone with a wine glass in her hand and I was shocked that no one was around her. But again, given that this was Paris, I probably had a higher chance of getting hit on than she did.

I had just recently been looted to fulfill the desires of my penile organs. You would assume that I would adhere to the phrase, 'Once bitten, twice shy'. But, a man is a slave to his hormones. So foolhardedly, I walked up to her.

"They say Paris is empty without romance, you know?"

She turned to me, "What?"

"Well, you know. Paris is all about romance."

She gave me a weird look and said, "You couldn't think of anything better?"

"Nope. Not really." I paused for a while and then said, "Uhhh… You're really pretty."

She chuckled, mocking my flirtation skills, "You look pretty decent. You're Indian, aren't you?"

"Yup. I am not very proud of being Indian, but I am from that country, yes. Does that help my case?"

She smiled and looked at me, "Not really."

I was surprised, "It never helps being Indian, you know, especially with women abroad."

"It does help that you are from that country. You don't make a strong case for yourself when you say you are not proud of being from there."

"Oh." I sighed and put my drink beside her. "How did you guess I'm Indian. Most people think I'm Mexican."

"Well, it takes one to recognize one."

This lady was whiter than most white people I've seen. She had flowing hair, and light blue eyes. Her English had an accent you could hardly call Indian. She was an Indian blessed with foreign features and tongue.

"Has someone told you that you look like Katrina Kaif?"

"Who's that?"

"You know, there's this new actress who's come in the movie *Boom*. She's also rumored to be Salman's girlfriend."

"Oh. If I'm Katrina and you're trying to be with me, that makes you…"

I immediately shouted out putting my collar slightly up, "Salman."

She chuckled again. "You wish. So, is your name Salman?"

I smiled. "Dhruv."

"Hmm…. That means a prince, doesn't it? You don't look a prince…A pauper would have been a more apt name. Your parents got it wrong, you know?"

She was taking my case left, right and center. "Yeah, well. I get it. I'm out of here."

She laughed and held me by my hand, "No, no. Don't get up. Sit down. I'm Katrina, remember? I'm entitled to my tantrums."

"Clearly. So do you have a name?"

"Well, yes. My parents called me Aisha."

"Hmm…that's a pretty name."

She looked at me and gave a condescending nod. "Tsk tsk. Still trying hard."

"Yeah."

She had the prettiest smile, seductive yet sweet. There was something particularly enigmatic about her. I couldn't really figure out what was it about her that I liked the most. We sat there for hours, arm-twisting each other. Time just flew by. It's amazing how words have a different effect coming from different people. It's not that we spoke about something very different from what I've talked to with various insignificant people in my life. It was just a random conversation with a girl who I was fascinated with. The best part of it was no personal details of any sort were either asker for or shared. It was completely random.

We tried to make fun of each other interim. Well, she was much better at it than I was. When we finished, I didn't get the end result I was hoping for, but I managed a probable next date. It was one of the rarest of rare times that I made it to the second date. I usually managed what I wanted from the first one itself. I left her home without trying to even kiss her. I imagined I would spook her if I did that. I did, however, succeed in getting her phone number.

I trudged to my hotel after that experience. I didn't take my usual serving of hookers that night and instead went straight off to bed. It was hard to explain why. I guess I just didn't want to get rid of the aura and replace it with a meaningless one.

The next day, I wandered aimlessly around Paris. There were people around with the typical artistic hats on them, and perfectly dressed. There was absolutely no one I could spot who was dressed shabbily. But the scenic foot-bridges, the lovely French women and the gothic architecture around me failed to really make an impression. My mind was pre-occupied with Aisha. I was wondering what would be the best time to give her a call.

I seated myself in a French café and ordered a croissant and some tea. I gradually garnered the strength to somehow give her a call. She picked up on the second or third ring.

"How are you doing?"

"I'm okay."

"I didn't expect you to call so early."

I didn't know the apt answer to the statement so I blurted out, "Well, I didn't expect you to pick up so early."

She instinctively laughed and I couldn't help smiling. I then asked her, "You know, that evening we spent together was one of the better ones I have spent till date. Maybe that's why you're called Aisha. Let's meet again."

There was silence at the other end. I started wondering if I had come on a bit too strong. After some time, however, she replied, "There's this nice restaurant Laurent. A lot of powerful French people dine there. Since you are a prince, I was wondering if you could feel alive with me there. That is if you don't conk off after seeing the bill."

I retorted back, "Laurent it is."

"7:30 p.m. today"

"It's a date."

"I am the traditional kind, so don't expect me to go dutch on the bill."

"No, madam. You won't have to. Your company is enough."

Laurent was quite the classy place, so I was instructed by Aisha to dress up for the evening. I had to wear a proper dinner jacket with a white shirt and the works. The dining room at Laurent was quite picturesque. There was a garden right outside and the restaurant had tones of orange and pink. The moon light shone on the leaves and the lighting was just about right.

Aisha was to meet me directly at the restaurant, so I went there early and took a table for the both of us. She came in wearing a white dinner gown; she looked divine. I was gawking at her for a while. She caught me staring at her and I realized that. I quickly glanced away from her.

"Damn," I thought to myself, "I should have bought her a corsage."

She reached the table and smiled at me. "Don't you want to welcome me?"

I immediately got up and pulled the chair for her to sit. She sat down.

"Wow," was the first thing that came out of my moronic mouth.

She gave me a look, "That's all you could come up with?"

"Well, you look just amazing."

"Thank you. You don't look that bad yourself, you know."

I smiled.

"So, what will the lady have?"

"Well, let's start with the red wine. The French merlot is quite famous."

She ordered some old red wine. The woman knew her wines. To be fair, the wine she ordered was not the most expensive on the list. It was quite reasonable compared to the other wines on the list. The waiter came with it and offered it to me to taste. I pointed him towards her.

She took a sip and made a look as if she was considering the taste, "Fruity, but it's quite smooth."

"You look like you've had a lot of these."

"I've had a lot of suitors across different nationalities. My job involves a lot of travel. So, I keep on meeting guys who want to take me out and some who I have to take out for official purposes."

"I can imagine."

"Well, I didn't cross propriety with many, you know. I am quite reserved that way."

"But you did cross it with a few."

She laughed almost teasingly, "Nah. I haven't crossed the line yet. I have kissed a few guys and probably had a little bit fun with a couple. But, I haven't crossed the line with any."

I looked at her and sighed.

She winked at me. "Oh, don't worry. I won't cross the line with you either."

I winked back. "That is exactly what I'm worried about."

She smiled, "You're still paying for this, you know."

"Yes, madam. I will foot the bill as promised. Like I said earlier, your company is enough."

She pouted her lips and nodded.

"So, I don't know much about you. What is an Indian woman doing in Paris alone? Do you have a family?"

"Slow down." She paused. "Actually, you know, let's not talk about these at all. This evening has to be something that you'll remember without knowing much about my past."

"So, I will never learn about you."

"We'll get to that in due time and cross that bridge if the need arises."

She didn't have much capacity or too much of a taste for a wine. She hardly had half a glass and stopped.

"For a moment there, I thought you were quite aware about wines," I said.

"Well, I don't have to be, you know. I just have to remember the two-three standard comments that people make. Most people just say fruity, smooth, etc. I did the same."

She smiled again. There was just something about that smile. It had that zing about it. I had never obsessed about a woman's smile before this. It was just perfect. I was down half a bottle of wine and a lot of breads.

We proceeded to order the main course. I think she ordered the lamb curry and we had some nice French bread to go along with it. I don't quite remember the rest of the cuisine. We chatted about life, existence and death, not necessarily in that order. We discussed money, ambitions and the lack of it from a third person's perspective.

Have you ever had a dinner with someone you don't know at all and not talk about yourself or her? For a while, you will feel that all of the past, including your fears, and insecurities, just doesn't matter. Not a word was exchanged between us about family. That conversation was the most interesting one I have ever had and one that I don't share much with anyone. It's a memory that is privy only to me.

The dinner ended earlier than I hoped it would. The bill wasn't as steep as Aisha had made it out to be. I took care of the cheque and we walked out of the restaurant. I did not want to go home because that would mean the evening would end.

"So, where do we go next?"

"We go home from here. You're dropping me home."

I immediately squealed, "No. I just paid for an expensive dinner in exchange for time with you. So, you have to now take me to someplace interesting."

She gave me a suspicious look, "You're not getting laid, mister."

I shot back, "No expectations for that, Madame. You made that pretty clear while we were having dinner and I made my peace with that fact."

She then looked at me, smiling again. "So, where do you want to go?"

"Take me someplace interesting. I'm a tourist, remember?"

"Well, technically, so am I. But, never mind that." She then pointed herself in the eastern direction and looked at me, "Come on."

I followed her like a puppy while she took the lead. She wasn't that big a fan of walking together. She would frequently outpace me. I managed to keep up with with her. She took me to a bridge with a lot of padlocks hanging on it.

I looked at her and asked, "Where are we?"

"You haven't heard of this place? I thought you were well travelled."

"I am not well-read or well-educated, you know? So don't be surprised."

"This is the Pon Des Arts…the famous love-lock bridge. You write your names on the lock and then lovers throw away the key down in the river below."

"Okay. So you've got a lock?"

She then stared at me, "We're not lovers, you know."

"Why did you get me here then?"

She pondered for a while, wondering what to do now that she'd got me here.

She then suddenly spoke up, "I wanted to do something crazy. So let's do this even if we are not lovers. You could be my potential amour." She then sighed, "Even though the chances are slim."

I ignored her last comment and said, "All right. I'm in."

We took a lock, tied it to the bridge, which had surprisingly a lot of locks on it. I was surprised the bridge had not crashed due to the weight of the locks. It was almost proof of the fact that love was the emotion which dominated the world and probably the one that made it go round.

She almost gazed a while into the night sky dreamily, imagining something, I guess. Her voice had a certain amount of peace which had an incredible effect on me. It soothed me and given that I was this restless freak, it helped me slow down time for just that little bit.

She turned towards me and said, "You know, a young woman in Hungary used to meet her beau here before he went off to war in World War I. She tied a lock to this bridge as a way of sealing their love forever."

There was something about that place. I just don't know. It was either incredibly coincidental or destiny that we were on that bridge together that night. She stared straight into my eyes and I was lost in them for a while. Her head moved towards me slightly and I instinctively moved forward to kiss her. Our lips met and I guess that feeling I had when I was kissing her on that bridge that night was magical. Our eyes were closed and the stars glistening in the night sky added to the romance. Maybe, this is why they called Paris the romantic capital of the world.

There had to be a touch of destiny and magic to the way I met Aisha. It was so meant to be. No kiss with any woman before this had been like this.

After a while, she separated herself from me. She wasn't embarrassed for losing herself in the moment. She was smiling and quite composed.

"Now, was this an experience to remember or what?"

I looked into her eyes, "Till me last breath, I don't think I will forget this moment."

We walked away from the bridge and started to drag ourselves to our respective abodes in Paris. There was not much exchanged by way of words. I guess we both were sort of lost in the moment.

We reached her place. When we were saying goodbye, I summoned the guts and asked, "When will I get to see you again?"

"Never."

"What do you mean never?"

"Well, this is all you have of me to remember me by. You're the reckless traveler. I'm your mysterious muse. If we find out more about each other, it will spoil this experience."

"I've already got your number. I will be calling you for a second date, you know. I am quite fascinated by you."

She then winked at me again. "Either that or it's your desperation since you didn't get to sleep with me yet."

"Yeah, it could be both, but that doesn't exclude the fascination."

That evening in Paris was an epiphany for me in so many ways. I look back at everything reprehensible I have done after that meeting, and for some moments, there is sufficient cause for my actions.

She will come like a breath of fresh air and change everything you knew about life. It is the moment when you re-define everything you knew about yourself and purify your soul and your existence

Love or something like it

"Why should I believe in love, Mom? The man you loved left you hanging."
"Love is a valuable thing, son.
It sets you free
I still love the man who left me
Love makes life worth living, son
Never stop believing in it."

I was stuck with her thoughts the entire next day and the day after that. I gave her a call and she didn't pick up the first time. I called again and the phone rang for a while before she picked up.

"Yes."

"Is this Aisha?"

"Yes."

"Dhruv speaking."

"The pauper?"

"I think you have me mistaken with someone from your last relationship. This is Dhruv, the prince."

"Aah..So why have you called?"

"Well, I think we have much to discuss."

"Your royal highness...I am but just a normal citizen. What will you discuss with me?"

"The weather, politics, travel, sitcoms and much much more."

"Oh..so you're asking me out on a date."

"Yes."

"So say, will you go out with me on a date?"

I sighed and swallowed my pride, "Will you go out with me on a date?"

"No," she said and banged the phone down.

Clearly, she was taking my case. I gave her a call. This time, she let it ring a bit longer. I patiently waited. After a lot of rings, she picked up the phone.

"Yes."

"6 p.m. Café de Flore, near your place in Paris."

"I don't recall saying yes."

"I will wait there till time immemorial, madame, like a pauper, and the moment you come there, I will transform into a prince."

"Aah."

"So you see I am much more a commoner than you, except when I am with you. You make me feel like a prince."

"Let's see. I suggest you don't wait too much. I might or might not come."

"Okay."

That was as good as a yes I was going to get from her. I felt like a teenager who had managed to get an awesome date. She was the first girl who made me feel this way. Before this, my relationships were mainly with members of the opposite sex who were similar to me in that they were looking for casual sex. This was different in that it involved pursuit, something that I hadn't engaged myself earlier in. It was quite crazy given who I was and what my circumstances were.

I was waiting for her at Café de Flore for half an hour. The café was very beautiful, much akin to everything in Paris. It had tables outside with an option to have an umbrella on top. It was rumored to be among the most beautiful cafes in the world. Apparently Picasso, Hemingway, et al., were regulars at this café. I took the liberty of ordering myself a coffee before Aisha came in. It was quite sinful. Piping hot, it came with its own refill. The café was also well stocked with a reasonable number of food options. I felt like ordering some French onion, but thought it would be better if I waited for her before I ordered anything.

I had so much to talk to her. I wanted to know about her, her family, likes, dislikes, work and so much more. A part of me felt that there was this mystery about her that attracted me. There was a good chance that once I saw through her, I would be able to actively pursue my goal of a goalless life and maybe the crush would be over.

I don't think Aisha was going to make it very easy for me to get rid of her from my mind space. She came that evening wearing a beautiful gown. The gown was laced velvette material, pastel pink in colour. And with her glistening complexion, it felt as if a fairy was walking towards me. She was beautiful, with a charming smile on her face, signalling something naughty was going on in her head.

"Madame," I said and pulled a seat for her, "you look breathtaking."

She looked at me smiling. "Chivalry ain't dead yet."

"As long as there are girls like you in the world, chivalry ain't going nowhere." She smiled that beatific smile again, and I lost myself.

"So what will you have?" I asked.

"A chocolate chip muffin and some coffee would be nice."

I signalled to the waiter. "Sire, could you get the nice lady some coffee and a chocolate chip muffin."

He looked at me. "For you, sir?"

"Her presence is enough for me, thank you."

He smiled at me and so did Aisha.

"You really know how to impress a woman."

"You bring it out in me."

It was a lazy French evening with amazing sights all around, but all I could focus on was her. I was smitten by her. I had made it a rule to never get romantically involved with a girl because that meant a relationship, and every relationship implied responsibility, curbs on my freedom and additional liabilities. I was quite dangerously close to breaking that rule that day.

"You haven't told me anything about yourself."

"I want to remain the mysterious muse."

I smiled. To a degree, the mystery part had me hooked. Maybe, she realized that too. I insisted. "Come on. At least, tell me something about you."

"Okay. Let's start about you first."

"I am a vagabond who's living on his father's money. There's enough to last me this lifetime. He's dead as far as I know. I've spent most of my life with my mother who's taken good care of me."

"Where is she now?"

"She died when I was sixteen. I was the only one she had. Ditto for me. I became all alone after that and somehow waltzed through my graduation. Apparently, she had left me a lot of interest generating deposits, courtesy my father, so I would never be short of money, whatever I did. I decided I never wanted a relationship or a traditional life given what I had seen what my mother go through, so I decided to chuck the rat race and travel the world.'"

"So you've got no aim, no vision and no direction."

"I've got no aim or direction, but I do have a vision that I want to stay across almost all countries before I die."

"Wow. That's one way of living your life. You're a hippie."

I smiled. "In many ways, I am a hippie. Now, let's talk about you."

"Well, I have lost my mother too, but unlike you, I did not get rid of all responsibilities. I started to work to help support my family and my father. I started working with this international fashion magazine back in India and worked hard until they found me good enough to shift here to Paris."

"That explains your good choice in clothes."

"You're sweet," she said.

"Yeah, like the wines you're so good with?" I smiled and so did she.

"I generally don't go out with guys like you, you know?" she said.

"What do you mean?"

"You know...the stereotype. Playboys who are discovering themselves by sleeping with many women until they find the perfect fit."

"I don't agree with you."

"Which part?"

"The latter. I'm not looking for the perfect fit."

She had the perfect smile, a 24 Karat one. You couldn't help but just look at her and be lost.

"Ever read the Harry Potter series."

"Isn't that for children?"

"No. So many of us grew up on that. Can't you imagine yourself in a magic mansion?" she said sweetly.

"Yeah. So many times, the wizard comes and he solves all our problems."

"There are so many problems. It's just the concept of having magical powers and living in a world where your only problem is a dark lord whom you know you are going to slay in the end."

"He loses a lot before he kills Voldermort. Are you ready to face loss?"

I stared at her with a blank look, "I've faced loss, Madame. I doubt if I have anything else to lose."

It was as if she understood what I was talking about. She smiled and changed the topic quickly, "It's always a battle of good vs evil, you know. At least Harry Potter knew he will win. In the real goddamn world, you might end up losing everything and yet you do not know if good is going to succeed over evil."

"Eventually, doesn't it succeed?" I asked.

"There are so many examples where the 'eventually' just doesn't come, you know."

"Name a few." We were again in the middle of a random conversation, which had me hooked to her.

"For starters, look at the Indian politicians. A lot of them have done so much shit, they don't deserve to live. Yet, they continue to prosper while the common, innocent man continues having a crappier life. There's no justice in the real world."

We had ordered some noodles by now. She took the noodles on her fork and was playing with it while she was speaking. She looked like a cute girl who was a bit of a know-it-all.

There were some photos on the wall. She pointed at one and said, "Now that was one man who fought for what was right."

My back was facing against the wall. I turned to see the photo that she was talking about. To my horror, it was the same man on my shirt.

I sighed and said, "Him again."

She heard me mumbling and said, "That's Che Guevera. He's a face for leftist justice. We need someone like him in India. But you don't seem to like him very much."

"Well, for starters, he keeps cropping up at various places. I mistook his face for that of a rock band player and an old man took it on himself to give me a lecture on how I should be inspired by Che."

"I take it you don't want to change the world."

"What change can I bring in? People aren't that great, you know. They ignore and forget you when they don't want something out of you. I am not a big fan of the world anyway. So, I really don't care too much about saving it."

She probed me further, "He fought against injustice, capitalist intentions. He was the architect of the Cuban revolution. Don't you feel enraged when you see something wrong happening?"

"I believe justice happens. I don't think I am meant to fight injustice. Also, no one fought for me when I needed it. I don't care if India is looted by its politicos or there's injustice around me. I am not meant to be Che."

She smiled and said philosophically, "You never know, Dhruv. Life can be very weird. It can change each and every fundamental truth in and around you whenever the hell it desires to. It doesn't take much; a few years, months, days or even moments for you to awaken to a new reality."

She did have some radical thoughts and even though I hadn't really seen the world and had no experience, I still had an opinion. I guess we all do.

I spoke like a snotty professor. "I disagree. Also, most of us are too lower down the value chain to be affected by injustice."

This was the first time I had used that slightly condescending tone on a girl I was trying to impress. Generally, I would just agree to whatever the girl said.

She raised her eyebrows since she didn't expect me to disagree. "You disagree, do you?"

"Yeah. There has to be justice in the world. It has to be natural. There has to be balance. Good has to win and right has to overcome wrong. It will happen. I do not have to push the envelope for that."

"I want that. But do you really think it's there? Do you believe that natural justice is a reality?"

"It has to be there for the universe and everything else to make sense. It just has to be there."

"Well, it's good to meet a man with this much positive energy. The other guys I meet have only negative stuff to say about the world."

"I'm a breath of fresh air, aren't I?"

She laughed. "Blowing your own trumpet, are you? You are an interesting man though."

"I know. I have said so many good things about you. As soon as you said one, I thought I will reinforce the notion." I winked at her, enhancing my cuteness quotient.

The dinner was nice and the company just made it brilliant. The evening ended and I offered to drop her home.

"You aren't going to be invited for coffee, you know."

I nodded. "I know."

"And are you okay with that?"

I looked at her with a condescending look on my face. "You've stereotyped me, haven't you?"

"No, no." She paused and pursed her lips, "Well, I've stereotyped you a little bit."

I smiled. "It's okay. Lots of girls have made that mistake."

I was on a roll. I was going to walk the pretty lady home with a clean intent that had been made clear right from the start. Given that I had been such a sweetheart, she had all the time in the world to make up her mind to kiss me.

I walked her home and on the way we talked about her life and her family. She opened up to me. It was a fifteen-minute peek into her life, and the more I came to know about her, the lesser she was a mystery to me. Generally, for me that meant a drop in my interest levels in the girl. This time, however, the more I found out, the more I wanted to know.

The road was quite full with tourists of different nationalities. Paris is always buzzing with people from all around the world, even late into the night. There are alcohol joints which are open all the time. The best part is, while you're walking back you can just randomly stop at a place and have some cold beer. There's a party going on almost constantly.

We reached her place. She was staring straight into my eyes when she said, "Thanks." I bent a bit to touch her lips and she responded. We kissed for a while and it was just the best feeling ever. She then looked at me with a slight twinkle in her eyes and said, "Good Night."

That was my cue. I wanted to leave from there because the night just could not get any better. I took off from there before she went inside her door. I walked a few steps and turned back. She was still standing, watching me go. She smiled and I smiled back.

When the mystery recedes and you don't walk away, the feeling of closeness begins. Butterflies were going up and down my stomach. I had never, ever seen a girl like Aisha. What a glorious waste of the former part of my life! I couldn't, however, be in love. I was too scared of the word *'love'*. Or could I?

Love makes living worth it, son. Never stop believing in it.

Life is a gift

"What will I experience when I fall in love, mom?"
"Nothing else around will matter, son.
Everything you do will be for her,
Every moment you spend with her you will treasure,
You haven't lived until you've loved, son,
She will become your whole world."

"We have to go this side to see Raphael's paintings."
I stared at Aisha with frustration replete in my eyes, "Seriously, I'm just here to see the Mona Lisa."

She gave me a pretentious look. "You know, idiots like you are wasting The Louvre."

"Really. You are quite arrogant about your intelligence, you know that?"

"Well, knowledge about the fine arts breeds arrogance. You wouldn't know."

We were walking the hallowed halls of the Louvre, with paintings to our left and right. Most represented a medieval era that I didn't know of and didn't understand.

"Wait, I think I've found the Mona Lisa. It says here that it's at the fag end of this lane." I dragged her unwillingly to the end of the lane.

For me, the earlier we saw the Mona Lisa, the faster we were going to get out of the Louvre.

It was a magnificent museum. I had never seen anything like this. It just did not end. Relics and paintings were everywhere. The museum had stuff from most eras. There were rooms and rooms which never seemed to end. There was a guide to walk you through it. The entire experience was actually quite enthralling. What made the experience better was that Aisha was with me and the fact that my making fun of the fine arts bothered her.

"You're not interested in other paintings at all, are you?"

"No. I just want to go back and tell my friends I saw the Mona Lisa."

We reached the end of the lane. I looked at the painting and then looked at her again. I repeated this procedure at least four or five times.

I paused for a while, shook my head, and then spoke, "No, you have a better smile."

She blushed at first and then made a smart face, "You have been searching for this painting just to pass this cheesy line on me, haven't you?"

"I swear I haven't. You have the prettiest smile I have seen. It is much better than the Mona Lisa."

She blushed a bit, hugged me and gently kissed me on my cheeks. It was one of those few intimate physical moments with Aisha. I had been with one woman for more than a week now, without any physical contact, and I wasn't missing it. Somehow her company was much more valuable than that.

"You're quite charming."

I took a bow immediately saying, "Am I? Thank you, Madame."

She held my hand and smiled at me. "I am now going to give you a guided tour of the museum and make you appreciate the paintings."

I looked at her. "It's akin to banging your head against the wall. You think you'll crack it, but you won't."

She sighed. "I think of you as a puerile man. But I do think you have potential."

She said that and dragged me across each room of the museum, giving me a detailed description of every aspect that she understood. I followed her around like an obedient puppy who would not dare to go against his mama. I shook my head and smiled at every detail that she shared with me.

There were one million pieces of art in the museum and I was scared that she might target taking me through the details of at least five percent of the collection.

After a long, long while, I mustered the courage to speak. "Aisha, can we go now. I think I'm already an expert."

She looked at me, smiling. "Yes, I guess we can leave now."

She grabbed my hand and guided me out of the museum. I looked at her. The way she was guiding me out of the museum, I almost felt as if I was her property.

She then looked at me. "So it was a holiday well spent, wasn't it?"

I stared at her. "That depends on what you call well spent."

She raised her eyebrows. "Didn't you enjoy?"

I retorted immediately, out of fear, or shall we say respect. "Yes, yes of course. I enjoyed so much that it felt this was the last thing I wanted to do before I die."

She gave me a look with her left eye slightly closed and then used the two finger 'I am watching you' maneuver to indicate that I better be careful. She also voiced it out to make sure I get the message. "You better be careful. I am watching you closely."

We then proceeded to lunch in one of those famous Paris diners. We sat down and ordered some wine and bread to start with. Good food was lost on me as all I was concerned about was what she was going to talk about and say next. I just wanted to browse through all thoughts that she had, everything that she felt and did. It was a new stage in relationships for me and I was warming up to it.

She started the conversation, one I haven't forgotten to date. "You ever think about death?"

"Where did that come from?"

"Here. See my lifeline is not very long. I don't know. It sometimes scares me, you know. I love my life. There's so much to do. I want to make a difference in someone's life before I die."

I looked at her and smiled. "Aisha, lifelines have a limited interpretation and are not linked to anything. You're an educated, smart woman. Stop fooling yourself with lifelines."

"Yeah. But aren't you scared of death? Aren't you terrified of the moment when we will exit this material world? Who knows what awaits us?"

I looked at her. "Not really. I doubt that I will ever make a difference in anyone's life. I am more a burden to society than an asset, born to lead a carefree existence till I die. Don't worry. I'm sure I'll exit this planet before you."

"You never get the feeling that you want to give back? You don't want to help someone and reduce the amount of injustice in the world?"

"I am quite incapable of doing anything that will help the world positively. I don't care about the injustices around the world. God has been just and fair to me. I might as well enjoy," I said and smiled.

The waiter brought our wines and we took a sip each. I looked at her intently. "You look like someone who will make a difference someday."

She smiled at me "Thank you."

"You also look like someone who will have a long and happy life."

She again smiled. "Awww.. Thank you so much."

For a moment, I almost had the instinct to ask her to lead her life with me. But, something held me back. I guess it was the intuition at the back of my head that she was probably not ready and I was not the right fit for a girl who was so motivated in her life. My career, after all, was quite demanding. I had to figure out various ways to make sure my existence was useless, while she wanted to make a difference. We were poles apart. Yet, I wanted her to be with me all the time.

I looked at her and sighed. She noticed that and said, "It might still happen."

"What?"

She smiled and winked at me. "Nothing. You want to order a second glass. Our first round is almost over."

"Yes, a second glass would be nice."

She called for a second glass while I kept on trying to figure out if she had interpreted my thoughts. This one was a smart cookie.

We were sipping our wine when she said, "Life is a gift, you know."

"I know."

"No one has the right to take this beautiful gift away from you."

"Agreed."

The evening gradually turned slightly more silent with some conversation here and there from the both of us. I guess we both had been forced in a corner to think. I was falling for her. I think she got that. It was in my eyes and quite difficult to miss. She was instinctive enough to figure that out and was probably evaluating the practicality of the situation in her head.

We ordered our food and I cracked the ice in the room by making some stupid jokes. She laughed on them and the evening gradually gave way to the night. It was our fifth date in eight days. I just did not want to spend time away from her and obsessed about her night and day.

I went to drop her home as usual. We kissed each other on the lips. She looked at me and asked me if I wanted to come up.

This was the moment of temptation. I could have taken her up on the offer, but for some reason, it didn't feel like the right moment. I looked at her like a puppy and gently shook my head denying her offer.

She smiled and kissed me on my head and retreated to her room. The stars were quite clearly visible in the sky and Paris looked more beautiful than ever. The air was a bit chilly. I got out of there on to the main street and saw the road side bars bustling.

I took a beer and sat down at one of the bars. My mind had achieved an increasingly noisy state and I was just not able to focus. There were many moments in my life that I had questioned what I was doing, but my defense mechanism ensured that these thoughts were at best fleeting. Today, it was not working. I was not able to quell my thoughts and my mind was going in a million directions. I guzzled down my beer thinking alcohol might slow it a bit, but one beer did not do the trick. I think I must have finished four more before my mind started to get a little numb.

I quit drinking right before getting knocked out. I somehow dragged myself up and took a cab. I reached home and crashed on the bed.

I got up late the next morning with a hangover. I managed to make myself a cup of coffee and sat myself on the table next to the window. It was quite a gloomy day and the sun was hardly visible. I was staying in a small studio apartment that I had rented for three months. The timeline was going to expire soon. It was almost time for me to move away from Paris and continue my sojourn.

As I sipped my coffee and tried to come to grip with reality, she kept crossing my mind and I kept trying to think of something else. I was courting a girl who I had little chance of hooking up with. I looked up and said, "Why would you do this to me, God? I was meant to never fall for a woman this way."

Clearly, God had other plans.

You haven't lived till you have loved someone more than anything else. She becomes your whole world.

Denial

"Will I get to choose the one I love, Mom?"
"It won't be right if you do, son.
The purest form of love just happens to you
You wouldn't know when love hits you, son.
For me, it was when you were born."

I didn't know what I was feeling. It was a pity I had no friends who I could talk to about what I was going through. It's amazing how I had been cordial to so many people, yet I had failed to ever acquire real friends. I guess my way of life, which was a conscious choice, had negated the possibility of my having friends.

I was so confused. She had penetrated my existence and left me directionless. It was so much better when I had no one to think about or bother about. Life was one big, long vacation. Somehow, it felt that it was now probably going to end.

Love is a very difficult thing to deal with. You don't know whether to move forward, yet you can't live without the person you're in love with. When you experience it, you might end up on a tangent headed on a completely different path than the one you were headed on. It's difficult to explain, but it takes you away from everything else. You challenge every boundary that you ever created for yourself in your head. All this is just for one emotional feeling which a lot of scientific studies describe as an impulse.

I called her up again the next day.

She picked up almost instantly. "Hello."

I responded with an eager tone, "Hey. How are you doing?"

"I'm okay."

"Listen, when are you meeting me tonight?"

"I don't know. I might go out with my colleagues."

"So, let's fix a time for tomorrow then."

"I don't know about tomorrow as well."

I realized something was wrong so I flatly asked her, "Is everything all right?"

She paused for a while. "Yes. Why do you ask?"

"You quite clearly don't want to go out with me."

She just said, "I'm confused" and kept the phone down.

I called her again many times that day, and she kept hanging up on me, every time. I was going crazy. Imagine a man with nothing to do all day, obsessed with someone. I was borderline psychotic.

What was she up to? Was it something I did? Did I behave inappropriately? Maybe, she expected me to come up and I didn't go. Was she insulted by that? Was there someone else?

My mind was going crazy. I didn't know what to think or do. I had a few drinks to calm my nerves. The problem however was compounded by the fact that the drinks actually increased focus. I kept on drinking with the hope that they would knock me out and my head would stop going through everything that it was.

In some time, when the state of inebriety had gone from high to extreme, I was in fact knocked out. I was in deep slumber. The '*Devdas*' phase had hit me stronger than I had imagined. I was on the fast lane to hell.

I was unconscious for about eight hours. The sad part was no one missed me. My mother's death had left me all alone with no one to care for and no one to do the same for me. I was lonely and I had never felt it until I had met Aisha and probably lost her as well.

I did come back to my senses a few hours after I woke up. I washed my face, cleaned myself up and decided to go and ask her why she was rejecting me. I was still experiencing a hangover and had been slightly melodramatic about the whole thing.

I knew the company she was in so I decided to head there. She was working as a consultant there. It wasn't far away from where I stayed, so I decided to walk. Her office was in a svelte building with a modern feel to it. It was quite fashionable, with glass windows covering each floor. One could almost see people working inside. The French clearly knew how to make extravagant architecture.

I went up to the reception of the building. There was a French receptionist staring at me with her spectacles dangling on her nose.

She looked at me and said, "Yes. May I help you?"

"I'm looking for Aisha."

She looked at me and said with a straight face, "Why? Is she missing? May I suggest that you try the cops."

I was quite surprised at the random wit shown by her. For all you know, I could have been a client. On the flip side, she was probably used to recognizing random guys like me and could clearly differentiate us from her clients.

To continue the humor was probably my best chance of getting a good answer from her. I smiled and leaned over. "She's been missing a while, you know, and I'm worried."

She returned the smile and pointed to the elevator. "Second floor. Let me first check if she knows you."

She gave a call to the second floor and Aisha came online.

Aisha was quite shocked apparently and asked to speak to me. I reluctantly took the phone from the receptionist, knowing very well that Aisha might ask me to leave immediately and forbid the receptionist from letting me come up.

I, however, took the phone anyway and in a subdued voice said, "Hey."

The response was quite firm. "What are you doing here? Go away now."

I did not know what to say and words were not really flowing well, so I decided to give a short and simple answer. "No."

She was not very surprised by the negative response without any explanation whatsoever. Given my randomness, she was probably expecting it. She sighed and called me upstairs. I smiled at the receptionist and gave her a thumbs up.

She smiled back and said, *"Amant fou,"* which I later found out meant a crazy lover in French.

I trudged towards the elevator and headed upstairs.

I reached the second floor and Aisha was waiting by the lift, ready to attack me with her sharp words and menacing look. "So, what do you want? I don't like personal calls to my office."

"Well, I just wanted to find out where I went wrong."

She looked at me and flatly commented, "Don't you think you look a little desperate coming down here?"

"Yes, I do. You are the first girl I've come so far for. I don't understand. I didn't misbehave or do anything inappropriate. So why are you giving me the cold shoulder?"

"I am at my office now. This is not a good time."

"So meet me after office. Shall we say 6 p.m. for coffee?"

She sighed. "Okay."

Paris has some beautiful cafes and I stationed myself in the one I was supposed to meet her an hour before she was supposed to come. I sipped my coffee, waiting for her to arrive. Time seemed to have come to a halt and everything around me was happening in slow motion.

She finally came reluctantly. We ordered two lattes and I looked straight at her.

"You're pushing me away."

She gave me a sad smile. "You are not right for me."

"What do you mean?"

"You are the relentless vagabond traveler with a pot load of inherited money, whereas I come from a lower middle-income family with a father to support. I'm lucky I got to see Paris because of my job, otherwise I cannot even afford foreign trips."

Quite non-chalantly, without a shred of thought, I blurted out, "What's mine is yours."

She got offended. "I don't need your charity. I can support myself and my father."

I immediately retracted my statement. "I'm very sorry if it came out that way. You can't push me away now."

"What do you want from me, Dhruv? Are you looking for a commitment? I don't think I can be committed to a man like you."

I didn't know what to say immediately, so I stood silent for a moment.

She smiled and asked, "Do you really know what you want?"

"Yes, I want to spend time with you."

"Dhruv, I may have to move back to India in a while. You have to get used to life without me."

"But we still have time, right?"

Somehow, the counters that I was offering were not good enough. She was staring at me while I was contemplating the ways to somehow continue what we had without any commitment. I had to first fight with my own ethos and persona before I committed to Aisha. She sensed that.

She smiled. "This has been a fun time, Dhruv. But we are headed in different directions from each other. Time to part ways, my friend."

"If you're off in a few days, let's have fun for a few more days. I won't bother you much after that."

She smiled and knew I wasn't about to take no for an answer, so she said, "Okay. We'll see."

I walked out of there with the hope that I would now get time to figure out if I could put the pieces of my life together and figure out is Aisha was a permanent one in the ones to come. I came out of the building and looked up to the sky and smiled. She had to know how my life would turn out after she gave birth. That was the only explanation for all the pearls of wisdom that she left me with.

You wouldn't know when love hits you. For me, son, it was when you were born.

The conversation

"What will I tell her when I meet her, Mom?"
"When you meet the one you love
You won't be short of words,
And if you do fall short, son
Do remember the potential of silence.
It will express what words can't."

Aisha had almost agreed to spend time with me. The next day, without any hesitation, I quickly dialled the number. It rang for a bit and after a while, someone picked up. There was silence at the other end.

"Hey."

In a muffled voice, almost indicating that she had been expecting my call, she replied "Hello."

Just listening to her hello made me weak in my knees. She had answered my call after all the drama that I had gone through. She asked, "So, what are you up to?"

"Nothing. You tell me."

"Well, I was busy with something. Do you want to talk about something specifically?

I racked my head to come up with a topic. I actually had called without any sense or purpose.

Finally I came up with something. "You left the conversation we had in the café unfinished."

"Right. The one where you said you need a Ravan to have a Ram."

I was articulate enough on the topic, so I started. "You need a villain if you want to have a hero. If you didn't have a Ravan, what would your God do?"

I half expected her to call off the inane conversation, but something kept her hooked. She replied, "My hero is not someone who will eliminate evil. My hero is someone who will be kind, and look at the greater good. He won't look for vengeance when wronged." She then smiled and said slyly, "He will also know some art."

I ignored her last comment. "Vengeance is about maintaining natural justice. There has to be balance in the world. There is a Yin for every Yang, good for evil and an eye for every eye."

"An eye for an eye will make the entire world go blind."

"So, you want to reform people by using love? You mean to say Ram should not have killed Ravan?"

"No. I am trying to tell you a hero necessarily is not the one who kills the villain. He may be the weakest among us, or the strongest."

I smiled slyly. "Yeah I can imagine a weak Superman or a Batman who weighs like 110 lbs."

"Hmmm…No wonder you can't understand art. You lack the maturity."

"Excuse me."

She laughed from the other side. "So, why did you call?"

"To finish off our conversation."

"Is it finished?"

"No."

"We just settled it."

"No, you concluded I was immature."

She laughed. I could hear her laughter. I wasn't about to put the phone down so soon. If I could, I would never put down the phone.

"Okay, let's talk about something else. Tell me about your mother."
In a somber voice, she asked me, "When did you lose her?"

I went silent for a while. Losing my mother had been the toughest thing to do, and I had refused to talk about it with anyone else. I had done a pretty good job of that until now. I wasn't about to talk about her on the phone. I was an escapist by nature and when things became uncomfortable or bad, I ran away. It was time I hung up.

There was no voice from my side.

I was silent for a while. I thought she would keep the phone down. I would have escaped from the conversation and later on could pick up another topic.

"Who did you talk to about her death before me?"

The questions kept coming and I had no answer to any of them. That didn't stop her from asking them.

I breathed heavily into the phone and replied, "No one."

"Well, then that's something that I want to talk to you about."

I was stunned. Relatively, Aisha was still not close enough to talk about such an intimate topic. She wasn't holding back though.

I took a deep breath and said, "I lost her fourteen years back."

"What do you miss about her the most?"

By this time, my eyes were a little moist. "I loved the way she held me close whenever I was scared or confused. I felt so secure, so wanted. It felt as if the world didn't matter."

Aisha had silenced down. She had opened a conduit. I wasn't sobbing, but the slight hesitation in my voice probably made my grief perfectly clear to her.

"I lost my mother early too. I guess we are related that way."

There was a silence from my end for a while. I finally spoke up, "Yeah, I guess we are."

I sighed and became silent again. There was no communication on either end for about a couple of minutes. Yet, she did not keep the phone down. Silence communicates feelings in a manner that voice seldom can.

I was borderline desperate to hang on to Aisha. The more I convinced myself that it was not the case, the more it dawned on me that it was. She was quite perceptive and caught on to this fact.

After a while, she said, "You're quite lost, aren't you? I, however, might not be the one you are looking for."

"How do you know that?"

She laughed. "Dhruv, you are a prince. I am the pauper. I deserve and want someone who's more serious about their life."

"I thought you would want someone who's serious about you."

"By the way," she said with a pause, "I will be going to India soon."

"That makes it even more necessary for me to spend time with you. We haven't explored Paris fully."

She jokingly said, "Would you follow me to India?"

I paused to think for a while. I hadn't been to India since my mother's death. Something about that country always reminded me about her and the pain that she had gone through. I had managed to run as far as possible from her memories by avoiding the country of my birth as much as I could. It was a country I hadn't fully forgiven yet.

She then retorted, "I thought as much. You are a man with fleeting interests, sir. How can you be stable in one place?"

I sensed she was about to keep the phone down and immediately blurted out, "Why not? I might follow you to India."

"Well, in that case, I am willing to meet you tonight for dinner. Let's make it an expensive place, though. It's not every day that I get courted by a rich fella."

"At your service, ma'am."

"Well, let's meet at 7:30 p.m. at Raidd."

"That's a gay bar, isn't it?"

"I choose the place, sire. I want to see if others want you. That might influence me."

"I'm screwed."

"Why?"

"Guys have never really fancied me."

"Let's try again. This time, I'll try and influence them. Let's see if I can change their mind."

"Raidd it is then. Let's explore gay Paris."

It was set then. I was to go on a date in a gay bar located in the heart of Paris. There was a good chance that Aisha was just having fun with me. I was, however, addicted to her.

Raidd was accessible via the metro, so we hopped on one and made our way to this place. There was no cover charge going in, but Aisha made sure that she maintained her distance from me in order to not look hetero, 'cause that wasn't 'cool'. We were let in by tough looking bouncers who first tried to discourage us from going in because we didn't look or act gay, but Aisha convinced them that the purpose of our entry was to find a suitable alliance for me. I doubt whether they bought it, but she was so compelling that they let us through.

The bar was two levels and there was enough lip action and cozy behaviour all around. Songs were blasting while gay couples got comfortable with each other.

Aisha took me straight to the bar and then stared me in the eye. She raised her voice a bit and said, "Look, I'm tired of you tagging along as the third wheel whenever I and my boyfriend go out. Find yourself a nice guy at this bar and discover true love and happiness."

She winked and distanced herself from me. I ordered a drink, all the while watching her. She pretended after a while that I wasn't there and started swinging to the music.

A huge, bulky French guy approached me at the bar. He asked me if I was alone. I immediately replied in the negative. I think he thought I was lying, so he waited in a chair next to me to see if a boyfriend comes along. He just kept staring at me.

By this time, I had got quite uncomfortable with him glaring at me like I was an object to be had. I was scared to get up, lest he followed me. I looked at Aisha with puppy eyes, almost pleading her to come back, but she was enjoying my predicament.

I began evaluating ways of getting out of there. Aisha was smiling. I got up. Immediately, the man made a move towards me and said with a gruff voice, "Listen, my name is Loic and I will be gentle with you." He then winked at me and touched my penis.

That was my cue. I gave him a pelvic thrust to get his arm off my dick. I then ran towards Aisha, grabbed her and rushed out. Loic started to run after me. I was quite horrified.

We got out of the bar in a hurry. I hadn't been touched by a male. I was quite close to being raped by one soon. We ran and Loic ran after us. Surprisingly, Aisha was a good runner, so we were able to outpace Loic.

He was shouting loudly, "Come back. I will show you the world. Don't be scared."

We did not turn back even once, lest we see how close he was and he caught up. We just kept on running, hoping he gave up. He eventually did give up, but not before shouting a French expletive loudly. As soon as he did, Aisha turned around and showed him the middle finger. The chick had a lot of gall.

We then strolled on the streets of Paris. We passed by a bridge and were right in the heart of the beautiful city. There were stalls all around us, with drinks from various countries. We sat down at a store. I ordered a beer for myself and a glass of wine for the lady.

Paris was never short of illumination. There was lighting all around us, with street performers in the night occasionally breaking into a dance or a juggling act. There was just so much life all around us.

That was one of the best nights of my life. There is a thin line between fantasy and reality and I swear I did not know what that was. I wish there could have been an alternate reality where I was one of those men who worked in a bank and came back home to Aisha every day. What was in front of me was a fantasy, and to realize it, I had to possibly makeover my entire existence.

She looked at me, a twinkle in her eye, and said, "Let me know a little bit more about you."

"Shoot, but you have to share the same."

"Favorite movie?"

"*Schindler's List*. Yours?"

"*Casablanca*"

"So we both have a passion for the classics."

She smiled. "You like a movie about death and I like one that symbolizes love. We are so different. That's what I keep telling you."

I realized she was pulling my leg and retorted immediately, "I can tolerate a *Casablanca*, ma'am. That's more than most guys would do."

I then paused a bit and smiled. "You know, no one ever bothered to find out about me like you have."

She laughed. "You're lost, my dear Dhruv."

"I am lost in all senses of the word. No one knows who I am or where I am. When a child is lost, some part of the child's psyche calms it down because he or she knows someone is looking for him. No one is looking for me. No one is going to come to my funeral." I paused and smiled, "I don't even know if I'll even have a funeral."

"You are in an enviable position."

I gave her an inquisitive look. "What do you mean?"

"Well, you are independent, free in all senses. We are all bonded by attachments, responsibilities and relationships. You don't seem to be bothered much by any of this."

"But my relationships have been superficial."

She smiled. "Well, you know, most relationships except the one that you have with your parents tend to be superficial. Friends tend to be fickle when their priorities change. Lovers tend to be fickle with emotions when the status of relationships change. There is very little beyond superficial."

I stared at her. "Is that 'very little' worth it?"

She winked, "Well, that's debatable, you know. Depends if you find the right 'very little'. Then, it can be too much."

As we continued talking, I lost track of what we were talking about. We were rambling on about life, love, loneliness and even death. We went on to talk about each other in detail, something that we hadn't done until now. I swear I sensed that she was interested in me when she asked me all that there was to know about me that night. Identity can be a funny thing. It had been years that I had hidden myself from the world, and had revealed it almost instantly in front of a girl I barely knew.

The drinks kept coming, and words kept flowing. Paris somehow looks more attractive when you're high. In a sloshed state, I managed to get a cab and dropped her home. When it was time to part, she ran her hand on my face. I sighed and closed my eyes when she did that. When I opened them, she wasn't there.

It was official. I was head over heels in love.

Paris remains one of my favorite destinations to date, but it's unfortunate that I do not have the guts to go back there today. I guess memories are a double-edged sword that way.

If you fall short of words to express love, silence can sometimes express what words can't.

Five questions

"How does one get to know a person?"
"You know someone when you know what he wants
When you know what he fears
His hopes, dreams, beliefs
How he wants to live and how he wants to die."

"What are your worst fears?"

"I guess it's related to losing my father. It worries me as to what will I do without him. Right now, he is the only purpose in my life. I'll be completely without cause or purpose in my life when he passes away. What about you?"

"I've already lived past my greatest fear, which was watching my mother pass away, quite early on. I guess once you've experienced the only one person who loves you pass away, you are not scared of much."

Aisha gave me a smile which sort of expressed to me that she understood and cared.

"So, who would you say is your favorite parent?"

Without any hesitation she blurted out, "I love both of them equally."

"Come on." I looked at her sheepishly, "I won't tell anyone."

"Well, you can't tell my mother anyway. She died long back. Dad has been alone ever since."

I had touched a nerve so I backed off, "Oh."

She then looked at me and smiled. "I loved my mother, and even though my father has tried hard to be both parents to me, he could never fill that gap."

"Right."

"What are you so insecure about, by the way? You just seem to never lower your guard."

"Aisha, even you don't let too much out."

She sighed and said, "Okay, ask me whatever you want to today. You're allowed five questions that I will answer in detail. These could be about anything."

"I'm curious. Why five? Why are you not allowing me four or six?"

"Well, I strongly believe there are no more than five questions needed to know a person. One should just know the right questions. We used to play five questions in school whenever a new kid came along and hence the number five."

"Okay. So I have five questions."

She nodded her head in disagreement, "No."

"What?"

"You have four questions."

"Didn't you say five?"

She looked at my perplexed face, "You're quite slow. Didn't you just ask me one?"

I made a disappointed face and said, "Okay. Now let's start with my first, uh.. second question. Do you believe in god and if so, which one? Lord Jesus, Allah or Lord Rama?"

"Yes and no, I guess. I don't believe that there is a god who listens to us when we are down to help us out. I do, however, believe there is one who maintains karmic balance. I think the concept of god should exist only to prevent people from doing wrong to each other. God-fearing people as a concept might be a route to prevent moral wrong doing in the world. I don't, however, ascribe to any faith in particular."

"Wow, that's deep, Madame."

She smiled, "Come on. I haven't got all evening. There's a nice dinner waiting for us at La Penn Quotidian. I won't answer questions at the restaurant."

"Okay. Have you ever loved before, romantically?"

"I have not loved anyone yet in the romantic sense. I have been in relationships, but they have been disappointing. The mindsets of the two men I have been with were misogynist. The relationships didn't last very long. I've had crushes in college and got proposed many times, but I guess I just picked out the losers."

"What's your favorite place in the world?"

"It doesn't exist now. It used to be my mother's lap. I would love just lying in it and she would caress my hair. She would always tell me how good she wants my life to be. She was so full of life and hope. If I had to choose one place to go back to, I would go to her. I don't want to be anywhere else. I just want to lie in her lap once again. My mother was my life and she took away a huge part of me when she left this world."

"What's your dream…as in what do you want to achieve in your life?"

"Happiness. I know it sounds crazy, but I just want to live my life to the fullest. I've realized I don't need a lot of money for that. I want to find love too, you know. I want to find happiness and peace in the arms of the man that I fall in love with. It just sounds too idealistic, but that is what I desire. I hope god is kind to me."

"I have a couple of questions more."

She shook her head in disapproval. "Game's over. You already got your five questions."

I made a cute puppy face hoping she would change her mind. Unfortunately, she didn't. We headed to dinner in this cute little Parisian café that she had booked a table at. There weren't many people there. It was a quaint place, La Penn Quotidian.

We settled down at the café.

A waiter came up to our table, "Will you have sparkling water or normal water?"

"Normal."

I looked at Aisha, "Some wine for you, Madame?"

She smiled, "Merlot for me, please. This bottle on your menu looks good, thank you."

There was mild piano in the background. I think it was Bob Acri. It was just perfect.

I looked at her and sighed. "So, I do not get my two questions, do I?"

She looked at me quite playfully. "You know, I just might grant you those questions…"

"If…"

"If you tell me your darkest secret."

"Damn. That was actually my question!"

"Well, I asked it first."

I cringed a bit and said, "When my mother died, my father did not show up. He had some joint accounts which I was unable to close. I forged his signature in those accounts and claimed the money in them, which was quite a substantial amount. He never came back for it and I would like to think he left it for me, but I never informed him, lest his second family came for it."

"So, you think you've stolen from him."

"Well, I tell myself no, but there have been ethical gaps for sure in the manner that I behaved. I've never been sure, you know. It remains my darkest secret, because effectively, I may have stolen from my father and I hated him."

She smiled.

I countered, "What's your darkest secret?"

"I had an affair with a man who abused and hit me. The day I left him, I was extremely aggressive with him. I hit him on the abdomen with a hard object lying there and ran off. I almost paralyzed him and ran away from there."

"Didn't he come after you?"

"I had some leverage against him because I had found out he was stealing from his job, so I sent him a mail asking him to stay away from my life else I would present some raw data of his robberies to his boss. There was someone following me on the streets a week after and I ran into the police station. We changed cities and I changed my job soon after. I guess he gave up after that."

"Wow. That's some story."

"Yup."

"How would you want to pass away?"

"That's the last question, sire."

"Yes, madame."

"By the way, you are seriously asking me to choose the way I will die?"

"Yes."

"Why would you ask me that?"

"I often think of the time I will pass away. I think we fear the end. We obsess about it and just can't make our peace with it. I want someone to tell me how he or she visualizes that moment."

"Well, I would like to pass away peacefully and hopefully in the arms of the one I love. I want to die knowing that there could not be more I could do for anyone in the world. I strongly believe we are here for some purpose, to fulfill some karma. I want to exit this world when that karma for which I'm here for is done. I do, however, hope that I will not face evil since I have not done anything bad to anyone."

I looked at her innocent face and sighed. I was falling for her.

She looked at me coyly, "The enigma is over, isn't it."

"Yeah. This is the time I usually exit."

"Then why are you still here?"

"I don't know. Seven questions are not enough to know you thoroughly. I will definitely need more time."

"Let's hope I'm able to give you that time."

You should know what he fears, his hopes, dreams and beliefs. You should know how he wants to live and how he wants to die.

I love you, Aisha

"Why do you miss people, Maa? I miss you when I am in school or when you are not around."
"People you love are in your thoughts, son
They form part of your existence
You are in every thought of mine
I am in some thoughts of yours
Love binds us, son."
"Should I tell the one I Love about my feelings, Maa?"
"Love is a beautiful thing, son
Express it at the first chance that you get
Such moments can be rare and fleeting
Don't miss them or you'll regret for the rest of your life."

I somehow convinced myself to give me and Aisha a shot. Maybe, it was my destiny to come back from a claustrophobic office to a home with crying babies and a doting mom telling me to go shopping even though I was exhausted taking crap from a man who doesn't know what he's doing and passing it down to me. It was possible to imagine such a scenario playing out. At least for the immediate future, it seemed possible. I was ready to go straight out of a pub to a household type of life.

Aisha and I spent the next week together. It was an incredible time, straight out of a romance novel. I learnt more about her and fell for her every day.

"You can't tolerate me at my worst."

I immediately retorted, "Try me."

"Love is about tolerating the other person's worst. Will you side with me through my worst moments, experiences and mood swings?"

"My mother suffered from leukemia. The last stage involved me as a sixteen-year-old struggling to keep her alive against all odds. All that made me happy then was watching her face. When she was going through her hell, the only time I saw her manage a smile was when she ran her fingers over my face. I made sure I took care of her every need and was at her beck and call."

Aisha looked at me and cleaned off a tear from my eye, "You're quite sensitive. I'm surprised you haven't fallen in love with someone till now."

"I killed that part of me after her death. I warded off love and decided to lead a vagabond existence with no attachments."

"How's that going for you?"

I looked at her and said, "It was going fine up till now."

"What changed?"

I smiled. She knew the answer to the question. It was a cold day in Paris. We were out in central Paris near some famous statue. It started to snow and the weather became a bit chilly. I spread my hands absorbing the moment.

"You haven't answered."

"You want me to bare myself and take the humungous risk of a reject."

"Yes."

I stared at her, stunned by the bluntness of the reply. "Seriously?"

"You come across as a scared cat. I want you to come out of that."

"What?"

"You are either already in love with me or you are in the illusion that you are in that state. Either way, man up and say it."

I stared at her for a while, not knowing what to say. The image of me coming home to crying toddlers came to my eyes. I thought of all the responsibilities which would come with those magic words, 'I Love You'.

She then looked down towards my crotch. "Are you sure you are a man?"

I was utterly confused. Did she want me to express my love for her? Was she at the same stage that I was? Was she pulling my leg or did she want a formal proposal?

She was right there in front me – the love of my life. All I had to do was ask if she saw any sort of a future with me. My mind was too warped to think straight at that instant. My existence had heretofore been that of a hippie, and I was not sure of the huge change that those three words would bring to my life. I was also quite encumbered by the fear of loss which had assumed control of me after my mother's demise.

I just kept staring at her and eventually sighed. She gave me a sad smile. She had just taken the initiative and I had not responded. It was that moment when I could have said it and even figured out the consequences later. I just didn't.

The rest of the evening just drifted away. It was a relatively silent evening, one that had me confused about what I wanted. She had been reclusive, but I guess she was as clear as she could be. She had hinted at all that I would have to give up and challenged me to ask for a commitment. Her cards were on the table; mine were close to my chest. There was good chance she would fold soon if I was not going to reveal mine.

I dropped her home that day and noticed an odd distance between us. I had the gut-wrenching feeling that I might not see her again, but she hadn't expressed it, so I kept convincing myself that it was not so.

The next day, I tried calling her, but to no avail. She did not pick up my calls. I thought it was because of the incident that had happened the previous night. At night, I decided to go to her service apartment, which she shared with two of her colleagues.

I reached the place and they were not there either. They were not from any registered company in the UK and were untraceable. She had vanished without a trace. I wonder why she would do that to a jobless soul.

A lot of questions crossed my mind that day. Did she really love me? Was she just playing around with me? Was I the stranger she met and had a short romance with?

"You look stressed."

"I haven't been having a very good day."

She just hugged me. I looked at her in surprise. She then looked at me and asked, "Feeling better?"

"Well, a little. But my heart's still a bit heavy today. I don't know what it is."

She then ran her hand over my face and said, "May god relieve you of all your tensions."

I smiled back at her. "Relieved."

We both laughed together for a while.

There was a reason why Aisha was pushing me to say those words the night before. She wanted to see if I could say them before I left. She wanted to see if I had the guts to commit to a woman I had clearly fallen for. She wanted to see I considered her worthy of my making all the sacrifices needed. Given the brilliant persona that I was, the answer was no on all counts.

It should have been easy for me to forget her. Before I had met her, I had had a series of flings. In fact, there were a few girls who probably felt for me. I hadn't considered that it was a big deal for me to walk away, to vanish, to leave without an explanation and sometimes without a goodbye. I asked the owner of the service apartment and he said that all of them had gone back to India. He refused to reveal the address, but at least I knew the city that she came from.

I thought I could get her out of my mind but it was difficult. I don't know what it was about her. It could have been the fact that her smile was infectious or that she was gorgeous beyond belief, and yet had no ounce of pretentiousness, or the fact that I had absolutely nothing to do all day so I needed something to obsess about. The possibility of the latter was the highest.

I decided to track Aisha down. It was difficult, though. For starters, she had gone to India, which was a country I wasn't keen on visiting. The other problem was that Wikipedia showed that Mumbai had more than twenty million people. It wouldn't be easy to track her down. Then again, I had a start. I knew the name of the company she worked for. So, I really didn't need a Sherlock or even a Watson to reach out to her. It would require some preliminary investigation and then I would be within kissing distance from her.

The first step was to make up my mind to go back to India, the country where I lit fire to my mother's lifeless body. It was the country where people showed a lot of love to the both of us. She survived a violent husband, a couple of attempted rapes after her husband died, and only her son's shoulders when she was taken to the morgue and burnt. She died in a country famous for medical tourism without much medical help and careless doctors. I had to make up my mind to go back to 'Incredible India'.

To this day, I regret not expressing my feelings at that moment when Aisha had instigated me. If there was an instant in time that I could rewind and change my response, it would be that one.

I love you, Aisha, and I was a fool for not saying it in front of you.

Express love at the first chance that you get. Such moments can be rare and fleeting. Don't miss them or you'll regret for the rest of your life.

Life and death

She held my fingers. I was barely sixteen years of age then.
I couldn't control the tears in my eyes, "You are leaving me, Mom.
Please don't leave me alone. I can't live without you. I will kill myself."
With some effort, she looked at me and said,
"The day you die, son,
The only aspect of me left in this world will be dead,
You are my life's work.
We don't pass away without leaving something behind, son,
The way to keep the dead alive is in your memories,
The way you live your life thinking about them,
Whenever you remember me, I will be alive again."

Aisha was found on the road, almost lifeless. Some people noticed her, and instead of calling the police, called the press. A journo van came to the incident before anyone else and they recorded the incident and immediately took her to the hospital.

Aisha was alive…barely though. It seemed as if the person who did this to her had assumed she was dead, but she was still breathing. She was struggling and somehow managed to stay alive while they got her to the hospital.

The news aired immediately and many other press stations rushed to the hospital. It was not just a case of rape. It was one which was brutal with no regard for law, order or anything else. People started collecting outside the hospital. There were women's rights organizations, young kids and some influential political personalities. There was noise all around. The news channels were only airing this incident since a number of people had accumulated outside the hospital. The more they aired, the more people came.

The situation also led to political overtures. Flags of the opposition party were soon seen in the mob gathered outside the hospital. It was a great moment for them. The law and order situation was coming under question and that meant they could raise a finger on the ruling party. Women's rights organizations had been under the radar for a long time and needed funding to continue their politics. A few young ones genuinely thought the protests would make the roads safe for them even when they wore western wear. Aisha's rape clearly meant a lot to everyone in India.

It was in that commotion that I reached the hospital. I had come to India on the 8th October, spent two days in figuring out where she could be and reached her house, on her birthday as planned. Unfortunately, when I went to her house neighbours told me she had been ravaged and admitted to a hospital.

It was just so sudden for me. A part of me just didn't believe it. It was not possible. Maybe the girl they were talking about was someone else. There was a chance that there could be another Aisha. There was also a chance that it could be some other girl who stole her identity. It could not be Aisha. I clenched my teeth and closed my eyes. It had been quite some time since I had prayed to god. I prayed hard that evening that the girl was not Aisha. But, god had never listened to me. I sort of knew that he was not going to start now.

Amidst the chaos, I managed to enter the hospital. There was a lot of media outside. They, however, had no clue of the perpetrator. The criminal was at loose and the media was thrashing the system in the country and the law and order situation. Politicians were being bashed left, right and center over this incident and talk of women's security in the country had become central on news channels that night. International media had apparently also taken note of this situation because globally there was not much going on. Unfortunately, there was peace everywhere else and in everyone else's lives.

I, somehow, reached close to the room that Aisha was in. There was supposed to be police protection, but given the amazing efficiency with which they work in India, there was almost no one outside. I took a camera out nevertheless, so that people think of me as a journalist, since there was a huge risk of the crime being pegged on whoever came near Aisha that day. I went in quietly with a camera and pretended to take photos.

She was awake and stared at me. There was a ventilator that was covering most of her face. I could make out the tears in her eyes. Her father was outside in a state of shock. I could hardly breathe for the time that I was there. I just stared at her and held her hands. Tears started flowing down my eyes and I was out of control.

She knew she was about to die. Her eyes, if they could speak, would have shouted out to me to save her. She pointed at a sheet of paper and I gave it to her; she wrote something on it and gave it back to me. I read the contents and put it in my pocket. For the remaining moments that I was there, I just kept staring at her. Her eyes were barely open and she fell asleep. There was a lot of noise outside, yet there weren't many who came to see how she was doing. Aisha's relatives and friends wanted nothing to do with this incident.

Her vitals were on the edge and it was only a matter of time. I have never experienced so much emotional trauma as I did in the ten minutes that I was in that room looking at Aisha.

I walked out of the room and quickly cleaned my eyes. The police were busy controlling the media. One of them saw me with a camera and dragged me out of the hospital. While he was doing so, I saw her father hitting his head on the hospital wall which was already quite red. He was shouting loudly and crying incessantly. No one cared to stop him or console him. The people who cared were outside with their banners.

I was now with the media and a part of them. I was dependent on updates of Aisha's health on official communication and any news that came to the media. I hoped against hope that she would somehow make it.

I quietly sat down on the floor near the hospital. It felt as if someone was watching me. I couldn't really spot who it was, but there was someone who was definitely keeping an eye on me.

Every moment that passed was a moment that Aisha inched closer to death. I could feel it while I was outside. I knew I couldn't go in again because if I did, cops would start asking questions and they were under a lot of pressure to find a head that they could pin this on. I so wanted to see her again. I wanted to sit by her bedside and talk to her one last time.

I fell asleep on the roads outside and was rudely woken up by a police inspector, "What are you doing here? You media guys will do anything for news. Go home to your wife."

I stared at him for a while and then blurted out, "Sir, I'm waiting for an update on the girl's health."

"She's fine as of now, but she's going to die in some time. We are telling the media she's out of danger to avoid any riots."

"Maybe she will make it, sir."

"How will she make it? That animal who did this to her has hurt her in her intestines. There are injuries all over her body. Even if she makes it, she will be a vegetable. It is better that she dies."

It was pitch dark and there were very few media guys around. I nodded quietly and stared at the hospital. There was a tree with some sort of a round seat surrounding it. It was empty since a lot of guys had gone home. I quietly sat under the tree and gradually fell asleep.

A man was on top of her and she was shouting. He had gagged her mouth and was gradually stripping her. She was looking at me for help and I was rushing towards her and yet, somehow, I was just not able to reach out to her and help. She was struggling and her eyes were shouting out for help. He was ravaging her like an animal. I couldn't see his face, but I just couldn't reach out to her and save her.

Someone woke me up in the morning. It was some media person looking for a place to cool off his heels. I got up with a jerk and was breathing quite heavily. The media person gave me a gentle tap on my back. It was an indication that my nap time was over and it was time to let others.

Some journalists had brought a copy of their respective morning papers with them. The papers were full of this news. The headlines in most said the perpetrator was unknown and there were various speculations on who could have committed this heinous act. Most fingers were pointing to random drunk people on the road and the government was under attack for not being able to protect its citizens. Some politicos from the ruling party blamed Aisha for not following the basic safety rules and for not wearing the proper clothes. They indirectly blamed the entire incident on Aisha. This was the problem with our generation according to them.

A politico, Mr. Ramesh Singh, wrote and I quote, "Women have gone away from their traditional roles and this has led to events such as these. Where are our Indian ideologies? Women have become corrupt due to exposure to Western theories. Their traditional roles were to cook, clean and take care of their husbands. Since they have deviated from them, such incidents occur."

I wished from the bottom of my heart that whoever the perpetrator was, Mr. Ramesh be hanged before him. Evolution took us from an ape to an intelligent, evolved human and yet, some people got left behind. I guess these idiots were scared of change. They were used to the concept of the Indian housewife and found it difficult to get out of the stereotype. It was probably not criminal to harbor that notion, but to say it out loud at a moment like this, when an innocent girl was struggling for her life and indirectly placing the blame on her, was an unpardonable offence. Then again, no one could do anything about it.

We were all outside, waiting for updates, and a kind soul came and offered me tea. This man was quite tall and it seemed he was probably the one who was watching me. I didn't have the energy to question him about it; add to it the fact that I had nothing to lose, so I quietly took the tea from him and thanked him without engaging in any conversation.

My mind was towards Aisha. Every time I thought about her, tears would come flowing from my eyes. I tried hard to control them since I did not want anyone to know I was involved. All her memories came to my head and I tried hard to suppress any and every thought about her.

There was a new development that day. Some women's groups and students accumulated outside the hospital. They had banners saying *'My Body, My Choice'*, *'Teach your sons how to behave'*, *'Death for the Rapist'* and many more. They started to accumulate outside the hospital and there were shouts all around. People had started shouting slogans and the media attention had now turned from knowing Aisha's health to the protestors.

There were barricades set up at the hospital gate preventing the crowd from going beyond a point. While there were many who had come there for a reason, the ones at the front were mainly trying to get themselves in the cameras and making a mess of the situation by trying to jump over barricades. Police had come there in good numbers to make sure the situation did not get out of control.

Updates on Aisha's health were every six hours, and most of the times, the only statement shared was: "Her condition is stable, but not out of risk and we are monitoring the situation". I knew she was dying, but the outside chance of a revival kept me going as well. Hope is a funny, funny thing. You hang on to it with every little bit of strength that you have, especially when it comes to your loved ones.

The protests got worse with time, and some people who were not even apprised of the situation joined these protests. These were people who were fighting the system and faults in it.

I was standing there all this time, waiting for some news that Aisha was still alive. My heart was racing up and down and the speed got faster when the doctors came out with an update.

Another day passed. Aisha was fighting for her life. She had made it now for more than three days after the incident. There was a desire to live, a hope that maybe things will return back to normal, a will to come out of what happened.

Finally, the evening of the third day, doctors came out with a paper in their hands. There was pin drop silence as people were all waiting for the final news to be broken to them. The death knell was about to be announced.

I was watching them with intent, as one of them said: "Following the grave injuries and damage done to vital organs of her body, we are sad to announce that she was not able to cope and has been declared medically dead."

That was it then. It was the end of the road. You know that hollow feeling you get when you feel you have lost everything. That message was supposed to be a cue for everyone to leave the hospital. There were going to be no more updates. I did not know where to go from there. I was lost and though many neutral observers would have said that about my entire life, I was really, really lost this time.

"You know what I think really makes me happy, Dhruv."

I looked at her with a smile on my face and said, "Me."

"No," said Aisha. "It's the fact that I am free. I do have responsibilities, but the manner in which I'm handling them is on me. No one questions me, thankfully. I choose my life. This crooked society of ours does not allow that for women."

"Yeah, I know. One of the biggest gifts that can be given to someone in bondage is the right to choose."

"Precisely. It is incredible that I have been lucky enough to get this far without any male spoiling it for me."

"You are bound to go much further, my lady love. You have a lot more to cover."

"Yeah, I do hope I have a long, happy life. Throughout my life, I want my spirit to be free."

I remembered her words and couldn't stop my tears. I guess, finally a male had spoilt it for her. Typical of my kind, I guess. I hope and pray to god that her spirit experience the same freedom she did before this.

I hope I had died before you, Aisha and I pray that your soul rests in peace.

The way to keep the dead alive is in your memories and the way you live your life thinking about them. Whenever you remember me, I will be alive again.

My daughter was my life

"Why do parents love their kids that much, Mom?"
"Your child is a part of you, son
Your soul, your entire being
You give your child's soul a body
He returns the favour by giving your body a soul"
"What if your child dies before you, Maa?"
"There won't be much left of me then, son
A lifeless body waiting for her end
While I gave birth to you
If you die before me, you will condemn me to death."

Once Aisha opened up about her life, she told me a lot about her life. She talked about her mother who she lost early on to cancer. I guess we reached a point where we talked about our memories to figure out what drove both of us. When you look back at your life, especially the part when you were a kid, you almost feel a pause, almost as if there's silence around you and you are aware your life has drifted by you. It is a part one shares with someone else only when you reach that level of comfort, I guess.

I don't know why I went to visit Aisha's father. I just don't. I guess I just needed to talk about Aisha, share my loss with someone who might understand. I wanted someone to make things right. But, I guess

I just wasn't able to fathom the magnitude of his loss and hence, his inability to share it with anyone.

▼

"Come, come quickly. Aisha is singing twinkle twinkle little star. It sounds like twintle twintle tittle tar. It's so cute."

"Don't make fun of my daughter. She's the best thing that has happened to the both of us. It doesn't matter that she's come out of your womb."

"Shut up. She's only three. This is the age to make fun of her. She's so cute and innocent," her mother said.

Mr. Jacob picked her up. "She runs to me as soon as I come from office. She makes my life worth it."

She was all of three years of age. She had gone more on her mother. Right from this age, she was fiercely independent and hardly cried when left alone. The only child of her parents, Aisha was the apple of their eye. She was the reason of Mr. and Mrs. Jacob's existence.

Mr. Jacob stared at her. "She'll grow up soon, and probably leave us for a job, a handsome young man or education."

Her mother quickly lifted her up. "Let's enjoy these years with her then. They aren't coming back."

Aisha was smiling profusely. Her smile would light up her parents. She always thought crying was a waste of her time.

There weren't many things she wanted as a kid, and she was quite content with whatever her parents gave her. An active child, Aisha found ways to keep herself busy without bothering anyone.

As Aisha grew older and entered her teenage years, her mother fell sick. She was suffering from blood cancer, which went undetected until the last stage. Aisha took all responsibilities of the household on her head, knowing well that this was the last phase of her mother's life. She started taking care of her father while studying.

Her mother's condition kept getting worse. She was once coughing blood. Aisha put her hand in front of her mother's mouth and then rushed to get a towel. Her mother caressed her gently and started to cry, "I've spoilt your teenage years. These are the times you are supposed to be having fun. Here you are taking care of your ailing mother. My years are over, Aisha. Leave me to die."

Aisha just smiled and sat down next to her mother on her bed. "Maa, the most fun I have is with Appa and you. I love you both more than anything in the entire world."

It was a difficult time for the Jacob family. They watched Mrs. Jacob's condition worsening. All this time, Aisha maintained her composure. There was something about this girl that was just superhuman for her age. She cooked food for her Appa and took care that her mother had everything she needed. While doing all this, she made sure that her education wasn't interrupted.

One evening Mr. Jacob was with Mrs. Jacob while she was awake. Aisha was in the kitchen.

Mrs. Jacob looked at Mr. Jacob with sad eyes, "She's going through a lot of pain because of me."

Mr. Jacob was in tears. "I know, but I can't do anything about it. With my salary, we can barely afford help. Aisha has been tireless and always by my side. God hasn't helped me as much as my daughter has."

Mrs. Jacob wiped his tears and gave her husband a tired smile. "God is helping you through your daughter."

"Don't leave me, Maria. I am not capable of raising her on my own."

She gave a somber smile and ran her hand over his cheeks. "No, but I believe she will take care of the both of you. My younger one will take care of my elder one."

Her condition worsened day by day and she passed away after a few months. The family was left stranded and all alone. Not many people attended her funeral. Their world was small and it had got a whole lot smaller. Aisha refrained from breaking down in front of her dad. He cried inconsolably while she controlled herself and tried to calm him down.

A few months after her mother's death, Aisha was due to complete her tenth standard examination. She somehow managed to get a decent result. She went on to complete her twelfth standard and helped her father by taking care of the home front. Her father was working with a textile firm and even though he wasn't paid very high, he was valued and they took good care of him.

Aisha got admission in a Bachelors of Commerce course after her twelfth. She worked hard in her studies and was a sincere student. There was a sense of self-belief that she harboured, one that wasn't very commonly found.

"Appa, I've got an offer from this airline. It is a management trainee position and I will be assisting the ground staff."

Mr Jacob hugged Aisha. "You are headed for great things. You deserve them. Normally, kids owe their existence and everything they have to their parents. In your case, your parents owe everything they have to you."

Aisha hugged him back and said, "No Appa. I also owe everything to you. If Maa was here, she would have been very happy."

"Which airline did you join, Aisha?"

"It is Spice, Appa. My last interview was with the owner only. He found me suitable for this position."

"Be careful of these rich men, darling. They can't be trusted."

"He seems like a good man, Appa."

Memories kill, especially if they are of a child that you have raised and lost. A child whose smile you've revered for the better part of your life murdered would generate a lot of emotions ranging from anger to sadness to downright depression and disbelief. For Mr. Jacob, Aisha was still the child whose creation was one of the best things he had ever done in his life.

I found Mr. Jacob in a corner of the house. He was sitting down staring blankly at a wall. There was no light in the room. His eyes were full of tears and there was no one to console him.

I went up to him, "Sir, are you okay?"

He hugged me and started crying loudly, "Why did god do this to her? He should have taken my life instead. My daughter was an angel. She did not deserve this."

I instinctively hugged him back, "I know, sir. I know."

He cried as much as he could. He got up and started knocking his head to the wall.

I stopped him, "Sir, please don't hurt yourself. You have to live to get justice for your daughter."

He stared at me. "What will I do with that justice? It won't bring her back."

"Sir, but we have to stop him from doing this to anyone else."

"I just wanted my daughter's happiness. I don't care if he pays for his sins or not. There is no justice in this world anyway. Bad things happen to good people. I have no desire for revenge. I have no desire to live. The only anger and frustration that I'm feeling is towards me. It is me who I want to kill. I was unable to give her anything."

"Sir, please calm down. You need to fight for her. Justice is needed to restore balance in this world. People like the man who did this to your daughter don't deserve to live."

"There is no justice, no balance and no god. You go away and leave me alone!"

I did not walk away from there for I figured he would take his own life if I left. He started to push me away from there. I resisted. But he kept on pushing.

"Go away." He shouted, "My daughter was my life. Without her, I want nothing. I just want to be rid of this useless body."

I kept trying to control him, but he was completely overwhelmed by emotions. I didn't know what to do just then.

He managed to almost get me out of the door. All through the pushing, he kept repeating one line, "My daughter was my life."

I couldn't fathom what he had told me. I hadn't had a child, so I couldn't for the love of god know what that man was going through. I hadn't raised a child from the time that she couldn't spell a word and looked at her eyes imagining the whole world through them. I hadn't seen her smile and cling on to me when she was scared or she saw a stranger. I hadn't experienced the sense of protectiveness one feels when a child sticks to you if a stranger comes near. And the worst part, I hadn't experienced the futility when your child is ravaged and you can't do anything about it.

Justice had to be delivered, so that balance could be restored. He was not the only one who was not at peace with himself. I couldn't get that god damn girl out of my head. Why did I have to meet her? I would have been happier leading my hippie life.

"What do your parents remember most about your childhood?"

"My mom used to tell me I was quite emphatic about my preferences, you know. I used to say no right from the age of two and they found it very cute."

I smiled. "So, people listened to you when you didn't want something."

"I'm hoping that will continue in life. I will meet a gentleman who will understand what I want and what I don't want."

I smiled and made a baby face, "You mean when you say Noooo."

I guess not many men understand a 'No'.

If you die before me, you will condemn me to death.

My body, my choice

I looked at the workers striking. "Do protests work, Mom?"
"A lot of them don't, son."
"Why is that?"
"Many reasons cause protests to fail, son
People protest for selfish reasons
They run out of patience and sometimes even a cause
Justice loses the battle
Unless there's a vigilante who decides otherwise."

I just don't understand why god blessed the male fraternity with a penis. It is a useless tool which should have been restricted to the job of just throwing waste liquids out. Animals like the one who did this to Aisha should have been born without one. On second thought, they shouldn't be born at all.

The protests continued and intensified outside the police station. The cops had no idea of the criminal till then. There were vociferous people outside the station, accusing the police of lack of security and blaming them for being clueless on the criminal.

It was the first time I had seen such protests. I did not understand their true purpose. But, it was possible that the protests led me to the rapist. So, I became a vocal participant of these protests. The number of people participating in these protests was quite high.

A lot of people got posters along with them. The posters said *"Punish the Guilty"*, *"Teach your boys how to behave"* and *"My Body My Choice."*

The police commissioner came out to address us. "We assure you that the guilty will be taken into custody and appropriate justice would be served." The crowd responded with shouts, "This city is no longer safe for women", "Fire the police commissioner", "You are all thieves who do not do their jobs well".

He went off escorted by policemen and that was all that we had at that time – an assurance from a police force which was not very effective in a country filled with a billion people and absolutely no visible clues on how the crime was committed. While the media protests and demands were quite steep and patience was running low, the purpose that the protests served was to make this a marquee case which the cops could not afford to ignore.

It was also a risky time because the police were constantly searching for a man to pin the crime to. At that time, they were under a lot of pressure and there was no way out but to present some criminal to the protestors so that the pressure could be released. If he was later found not guilty, the protests and hence the pressure would have long died down.

If they ever found out I was related to Aisha in any way, they would make me hang for sure. It was easy to blame any guy related to her and build a story around it. I had to stay in the clear and be careful about keeping myself as low profile as possible. No one knew about my relation with Aisha and I intended to keep it that way.

The protests started outside, with things worsening and random acts of violence. There was a lot of media covering the event. The police started to use tear gas. They also attacked the mob with sticks. I received a couple of blows and moved backwards to avoid any further blows and stay away from the tear gas.

A decent amount of people stayed there. It felt good that so many people were fighting for justice. The feeling, however, did not last long.

One man was approached by the media. The journalist asked him, "Why are you protesting?"

"The system is really bad."

The media person asked him, "Did you know the girl who was raped?"

He pretended to know the answer and said, "A fearless girl was raped today. I know that she will fight it out and survive."

The journalist was a bit disappointed with the revert since Aisha was already dead. He left him and went on to the next protestor. No one had bothered to find out much about the girl who was raped.

The intent of the protests, though, was good. They wanted to express frustration against sexual assault. India had, lately, started to become a country which was notorious for this.

The execution, however, was wayward. This was because of multiple groups present with varied interests. Some were blatantly driving an agenda. At one point, I noted a poster asking the chief minister to resign. There was a group of people who wanted the council of ministers dissolved and the prime minister to resign.

I was silent for a while. The police then came to disperse the crowds and started to send us home. We stood there for a while but were pushed away by a constable with his stick who said, "Go home. You will know when they have been caught. Come back then."

Someone approached me in the middle of these protests, "The establishment sucks, you know." I looked at him with a puzzled look implying the question, "Do I know you?"

He was a tall guy who seemed to have picked me out in the crowd. "They won't give any result to this."

I stared at him and asked, "What?"

"They won't give any justice to her."

"How do you know?"

"You have to wait and watch, I guess. I do know that you, especially, want that justice be served."

He walked away while I stared at him with a shocked look. "Why the hell would he say that? How did he know about me and Aisha?"

Once the main set of protestors went home, the on-ground activities stopped. The media coverage on the case continued with pressure being built up on the police officials.

Media reports were not restrained. They described the condition of the victim quite graphically. Every day involved a recap of the rape and the progress of the case.

Her father probably died a thousand times every day with almost every passer-by wanting to express their sorrow for the girl who was now a central part of mainstream media.

Mahatma Gandhi was the one who made peaceful protests popular in the country long back. But I guess the Britishers were better than the current lot of Indian politicos and servicemen in that there was some result of the protests. Finally, they left India.

Satyagraha was not as effective now as it used to be in Gandhi's time. It was fodder for media who used it to fill up front pages. One would assume media is creating pressure. However, there was no effect of any protests on any man in the administration in the current time. They were only patiently waiting for the next issue. Media outbursts had become common. With so many channels and newspapers, they were always looking for an issue to pick on.

The protests could have continued, but they didn't. We were attacked with tear gas and water. Elections were near and the ruling party did not want a spectacle like this on the roads. Meanwhile, something weird happened. A PIL (Public Interest Litigation) was filed on a ministry for not auctioning a public commodity. The value of auctions could have apparently run to thousands of crores. When compared with that news, Aisha was yester generation's news.

To be fair, the issue didn't die out completely. It started getting relegated to different sections of the newspaper. I used to scan the papers daily after Aisha's death to search for any news on her. I wanted to know who the culprit was. I wanted some closure and there was none forthcoming.

There was news of Aisha's father committing suicide which made it to the third page of the newspaper. He just didn't see any sense in continuing with his life. When I read the news, I closed my eyes for a while and imagined myself in that man's position. I cried my heart out. How does one imagine the pain that a father goes through when his daughter is taken from him?

The entire family was now no more. There was no one with enough locus standi in this case except me and possibly the law itself to take revenge for what had happened.

I was helpless. I couldn't push for justice, yet I wanted to do something. I wanted revenge so badly. But, I was a gutless bastard just as I was born. I guess I kept on talking about balance because I wanted nature and justice to make sure everything was fair. But it wasn't. Aisha's father recognized that he was going to be able to do nothing as well. At least he was able to get over the fear of death and take the next step. I was a coward, a sinner.

My emotions would take me from one edge of the spectrum to the other. I experienced anger, regret, sadness and almost every emotion associated with loss. There were moments when my eyes would be filled with tears and I wouldn't notice.

There were so many moments of solitude in India. I was borderline psychotic. My existence just did not make any sense. It was arbitrary. I had no purpose, no reason to be here. Any love I experienced was dead and no one knew I existed. Sometimes, I would shake to the thought of what happened to Aisha and shout loudly. I wish I had someone to tell me everything would be okay. I wish there was someone who told me he had my back.

I had no one to talk to or check the progress of the Aisha case. The case was pretty much dead and buried for quite a while.

I decided to do my own investigation discreetly. I tried to track down her movements on the day of the rape. I took out all news reports that said anything about the case, including where she was last seen, who she was last with, etc. There was very little to go on, but I thought there had to be something. I started to talk to people who had seen her that fateful day to get some leads on the murder. There was a guy spotted over her body. I was not able to locate that man because of the faint descriptions given by people.

Luckily, in the times to come, the police commissioner made a gaffe somewhere else and one of the popular newspapers decided to recall his failures which included the Aisha case. That gave some air to the case.

One day, there was news in the papers that the criminals had been caught. Apparently, a drunk rowdie named Bhim had been arrested for the case. The police claimed to have cracked the case and there were officers talking to the media about the diligence of the police commissioner.

From the day that I knew of Aisha's demise, I had never had a moment of happiness. My mind was going crazy and was completely out of my control. I heaved a sigh of relief. Finally, my head would get some peace. I wanted closure and I wanted to move on. Maybe once I saw her killer punished, my mind would silence down. I had nightmares of her being raped and me being there and not being able to do anything about it. Maybe after the perpetrator was taken to the gallows, I would be able to go back to who I was and get Aisha out of my head.

Justice loses the battle unless there's a vigilante who decides otherwise

The truth always comes out

"Do people hide the truth, Mom?"
"The truth stays hidden a lot, son
People say it comes out sooner or later.
If it does come out later than sooner
It may not serve its purpose."

Bhim had committed a heinous crime and had to be put away. I had decided to attend all the sessions that were held in court. I wanted to see him punished and see the entire thing through. The surprising part was that a case which had led to protests all over to this magnitude was not well-attended at all. There were a handful of people who had come to the trial. The attendees were mostly law graduates there to further their knowledge of the law.

Once the criminal was caught, the papers were full of stories as to how the police had narrowed down to Bhim. I read everything carefully. The evidence somehow reached the newspapers before it reached the courts. Apparently, he had been spotted in the area drunk by someone who knew him. He had a history of physical violence and had been in jail a couple of times before for assaulting women. He had no family and had been missing after the day of the incident.

The police found him after a lot of difficulty. He was not in his village and had taken off, apparently to the neighboring district. They had placed posters of wanted in and around the place of the incident and someone informed them after a week of putting the posters up that he was spotted in the area.

The police immediately reached to the place of spotting and Bhim was caught a few hours later. The media had declared Bhim to be a rapist-murderer and they made a convincing case. I wanted Bhim to burn in front of my eyes, but that was probably not going to happen. I guess if the law got to him and he was hanged, there would be at least some degree of justice.

There was a fast track court set up for this case. The ruling party wanted some sort of a decision before the elections so that they could use it as a brownie point. The legal process in India was apparently governed by the Criminal Procedure Code which had been adopted from decades earlier, and apart from the amendments in ethos, had been the same for years. It was extremely slow for this case and this was a fast track court.

Charges were framed quickly against Bhim. I had decided to hold my adventurous life for a year because I wanted to see this through. The hearings were public, so anyone could attend. Once the charges were filed, the case was set up for hearing quite quickly.

In the first hearing, the prosecution was asked to read out the charges against Bhim. He was charged on many counts, including rape, murder, and assault. The case began with arguments and counter-arguments from both sides. Witnesses were summoned one, by one including the men who saw him there.

I had little knowledge of the law, so after each hearing, I would try to go home and read about what I had heard. Courtesy the case, I read the Criminal Procedure Code, the Indian Penal Code and started to get acquainted with the law.

Some statements were quite enlightening.

"Every person is innocent until proven guilty and a case is filed only when there is an affected interested party."

At many points, the case would digress with the defense, Mr. Yadav making ridiculous arguments. I remember one monologue of the defense in particular.

"Your Honour, may it be noted that the girl was in a deserted place at night, so she was probably there to sell herself. No good family girl will venture out at this time of the night. My daughter would have her limbs broken if she dared to. Her father also probably didn't care. He lost his wife early. There is a good chance that he used her for sex and didn't mind her selling her body. These people are not right. My client is innocent and should be acquitted. Moreover, the DNA evidence is completely non-conclusive. The girl's father should be put into jail for this, your honour."

Mr. Yadav didn't bother to find out if Aisha's father was alive or not. At that point, I wanted Yadav to be hanged. The world was such a fucking convoluted place with men like Yadav. Bhim was obviously guilty and needed to be punished. He was instead attacking Aisha's character.

The prosecution lawyer, Hussain was lucky the public sentiment was against Bhim. He was a reserved man, one who didn't belong to the profession of law. His personality was not overbearing, quite unlike Yadav, who was a monster both in looks and demeanour.

The trial was able to garner media coverage. Media made sure that Bhim was declared guilty even before the trial. Everything about the story was perfect and the "Sherlocks" in the media had it figured out.

People hated Yadav. On one occasion, an agitated girl approached him and slapped him hard on the face. Yadav was in shock. He did not react. He just took off without saying a word while the media outside made a huge issue out of it.

I decided to do my bit to convince Yadav to let the case go easy. The day he got slapped, I followed him. He took off straight to a bar alone.

He was sitting on a table all alone when I walked up to him.

I went up to him and asked him, "Can I join you?"

He was surprised at a stranger being so forward with him. He immediately responded, "No."

I sat myself down anyway.

He was too frustrated to pick up a fight so he just gave me a look. "What the hell do you want?"

"I just want to have a light-hearted conversation about the case."

"I don't want to talk about it."

"I doubt you have that choice anymore given that you've taken the case."

"Yeah, I do. Get lost."

I didn't pay any heed to his argument and sat down next to him. He was too tired to fight, leave or protest.

He gulped his drink down and looked at me straight in the eyes. The setting was quite dark and the bar we were in was quite shady. It was a *desi adda* and the menu wasn't very fancy. I found a drink that was consumable from the bar menu and placed my order with the waiter.

"You look sad that you got slapped today."

Yadav stared at me. "None of your business."

He was two drinks down. My conversation with Yadav could have very easily turned into a brawl and I was actually not averse to that alternative.

My drink came quite fast. Yadav had gone quite silent. I took his glass and poured half of my drink in it. He rejected it at first, but then gulped it down and looked at me.

He gave a sad smile. "It's not the first time I've been slapped."

"Why are you defending that animal?"

He looked straight at me and asked, "How are you so sure he did it?"

"All evidence is against him."

"All of it is circumstantial. It could very well be someone else."

"No, it's him. I want him to be punished."

"You want someone punished, like all those people out there. Some want Bhim to hang because they believe the streets will be safer, some like you want him to hang so that you can sleep at night knowing Aisha has been avenged. You people want a scapegoat and not the truth."

"What's the truth?"

"I don't know, but this trial is one way to find out. Our legal system presumes innocent until proven guilty. My job is to defend Bhim and the truth will come out. The media has not allowed me to do my job well."

"Why did you attack her character?"

"That could also be the truth."

That statement got my blood to boil. I got up from the chair and held him by his collar. He was quite taken aback and my eyes went red. I was staring directly into his eyes.

Yadav was too shocked to react and in the scariest of tones possible, I warned him, "Don't attack her character or someone will be prosecuting me in a murder case soon. Let Bhim get what he deserves."

I walked out of the bar after that. People around were staring at me, but. I didn't care.

At the gate, I heard Yadav's voice, "I'm not scared of you. The truth will come out."

I kept walking without turning back. For me, the truth was crystal clear and Bhim needed to pay for his sins.

If the truth does however come out later than sooner, it may not serve its purpose

Good always
wins against evil

"Our teacher today taught us good versus evil, Maa. She said good always triumphs over evil."
"Dharam vs. Adharm is a neverending battle, son
It has been so for millions of years.
The battles in books always end with good winning over evil
I want you to believe that.
That belief, my son, even if it's not true
Will keep you on the side of the right."

Yadav saw me in court the next day and stared at me for a while. He then looked away and started to focus on the case.

The prime witness, Anshu Jain, who had placed Yadav on the scene, was summoned to the witness stand.

The prosecution, Hussain, started examining the witness.

"What's your name?"

"Anshu Jain."

"What were you doing at the place of the incident on the night of the crime?"

"I was going home after an outing with my friends."

He showed a picture of Aisha and pointed towards Bhim, "Did you see this man next to Aisha's body?"

"Yes, I did."

"What was he doing there?"

"He was staring at her body."

"Why was he standing there?"

"I don't know, sir."

"Was he making sure she was dead?"

"Yes."

The examination was not convincing at all. The questions seemed quite direct and the prosecution was not interested in going in the detail of the testimony.

The prosecution concluded with regards to the witness and Yadav was asked to cross-examine.

"Where do you stay, Mr. Anshu?"

"Andheri."

"Where were you coming from that night?"

"Dadar."

"How late was it in the night?"

"12:15 a.m."

"Where did you see my client and the victim's body?"

"I saw it in a lane in Bandra. I was passing by and noticed something strange in a lane. I stopped and turned my car towards the lane."

"What happened then?"

"I saw this man standing over a woman's body. I immediately took off from there and informed the police."

"What was he doing there?"

"He was standing there."

"That's all?"

Anshu nodded his head and Yadav continued, "Did he see you?"

"I think so."

"Did he run?"

"No."

"Did he just stand there?"

"Yes."

"Was he watching her, you know, in a disgusting sort of way?"

"I don't remember."

"Were you sober?"

"Yes."

"Doesn't it surprise you that the accused did not run away from the scene? He was, according to this witness, just standing there. What was he doing standing there? Was he waiting for someone to arrest him?"

The prosecution immediately got up, "Objection. He is leading the witness."

His objection was sustained. But, it definitely got me thinking as to what was Bhim doing there. If he raped Aisha and was done with the act, he would have gotten away from there as soon as possible. He didn't do that, instead he stood there. I was contemplating various possibilities, including ones where Bhim was drunk, or a sadist who liked to stare at his victim.

"Was the lighting good?"

"Not really."

"Was he drunk?" the defense continued.

"I don't remember."

"Were you drunk?"

"No."

The defense immediately went back to his table and picked up a file, "We have a testament from a witness saying you were drunk that night. Are you lying?"

"I had a couple of drinks, but I was in my senses."

"I have proof that you had a minimum of four."

The witness was sweating. He looked at the prosecution hoping for some help, but to no avail.

Yadav raised his voice, "Did you or did you not have more than four drinks?"

"Yes, I did."

He then turned towards the judge, "How can you be sure of this witness, sir? He was not in his senses. There is a good possibility that he mistook both Aisha and my client. Moreover, it was late in the night with bad lighting. He clearly cannot be trusted."

The courtroom fell silent. The defense had done his homework and the prosecution was pretty much left dangling with the credibility of its prime witness in question. I thought Hussain would cross-examine him to gain some upper hand in the argument, but nothing of the sort happened. Hussain just looked disinterested.

Character witnesses were then summoned and the prosecution started to attack Bhim's character. Hussain got a lot of help there. Bhim's character had been quite shady in the past. He had faced charges of rape, murder, theft, criminal intimidation, etc., earlier as well.

The defense did its best, but overall, Bhim came out like a villain who should not be out there on the streets. Yadav's attacks got lesser vicious as the trial progressed. He knew he would not be able to defend Bhim's character.

He did, however, when his turn came call out for the investigating officer.

"How did you suspect Bhim?"

"We had enough evidence that he was at the scene of the crime."

"Did you try and investigate other possibilities?"

"Yes."

"Who were the other people investigated?"

The officer started to ponder, "There were a few, but I can't remember."

Yadav's face grew red. "What do you mean you can't remember? Here, a man's life is on the line and no alternate possibilities were considered for the crime committed."

"The evidence against him was quite strong."

"What evidence?"

"He was seen standing there and his past was shady."

Yadav was getting angrier by the moment. He would have almost slapped the officer if he could. "Are you joking? That's the evidence you have? Did you do a DNA test?"

"No."

"That is standard protocol, isn't it?"

"Yes."

"Why wasn't it done then?"

The investigating officer went silent for a while and then commented, "We believed we had sufficient evidence to get Bhim."

Yadav said, "You did not even do a DNA test and on flimsy evidence, arrested Bhim. Are you guys sure you did the right thing?"

The investigating officer went silent.

He then thought for a moment and shot back, "Maybe you people conducted a DNA test and hid the results because it proved him innocent."

He then looked at the judge and said, "Sir, I want a DNA test done."

The investigating officer replied, "That may not be possible."

He looked at him and asked, "Why?"

"Sir, the body was handed over for cremation and is not with us anymore."

Yadav, to his credit, did not forge a defense. He did not call any witness to falsely testify to Bhim's location. He only focused on the lack of facts and attacked the prosecution.

I still remember Yadav's closing, "Is Bhim guilty of his past being what it is? Yes, but he is not guily of this crime. The prosecution has only focused on his character and presented flimsy evidence otherwise. There is no DNA test match that should have been done. Maybe the police did do it and hid the results from us. It is standard protocol. There is nothing that points to Bhim having committed this crime. You can't punish a man based on the fact that he had a regrettable past and that he was standing at the scene of the crime. The media has branded him a criminal much before your honor has passed a decision."

It made sense. The evidence was weak, in my opinion. It was also stupid not to have done a DNA test.

The pressure on the judge was immense, given the fact that public and then the polity had taken special notice of the case. Bhim was someone who no one except Yadav wanted to save.

It was the tenth hearing where the final decision was due to be given. It had been six months and I had followed this case judiciously. I wanted closure so I could move on with my life. For six months, Aisha and this case had pretty much become my life.

We were eagerly waiting for the decision on the day of the tenth hearing. The judge walked in. I was seated and Yadav gave me a cold stare as he passed by. I ignored it because I had a lot more on my mind.

The judge sat down and summed up the case in front of him. At the end of his concise summary, he said, "In the matter of the republic of India vs. Bhim on the count of section 375 of the IPC Rape of Aisha, I find the accused guilty. On the count of section 304 of the IPC – Murder of Aisha, I find the accused guilty."

I heaved a sigh of relief. Finally, there was some justice to the brutal rape and murder of the girl I loved. Bhim got what he deserved and I got my revenge.

We all got out of the courtroom and I was about to catch a taxi when a hand rested on my shoulder. I turned around and was shocked to see Yadav.

He smiled. "You need to give me five minutes now, so I can talk."

I let the taxi go. I owed the man this much.

The taxi went off and he dragged me off to a cigarette shop. He asked for two cigarettes, offered me one. He lit his cigarette, took a puff and then looked at me, "You think your revenge is complete?"

I smiled. "Yes, I do."

He smiled back. "You know, it's easiest for people like Bhim to be put into jail."

I shot back, "They deserve to be put away."

He smiled and then said, "I don't regret losing this case."

I gave him a smug smile. "I'm not surprised. You probably wanted fame, which you got."

He laughed. "No, no. I didn't want fame. I just wanted one thing. I wanted the truth to come out."

"It has come out."

He laughed again and then stopped. He then took a puff again, the smoke coming straight to my face, "Bhim did not rape or kill your girlfriend."

I stared at him. "What do you mean?"

He smiled. "I'm sure he did not rape or kill your girlfriend. I proved your prime witness wrong."

I shook my head and pressed the cigarette butt to the ground. I then threw it away in the dustbin and looked at Yadav. "I don't have to hear this. My job, here, is done."

I started to walk away. He held my shoulder. I almost moved to hit him on his face when he blocked me and said, "He told me the truth. I know when a person is lying. Bhim did not rape or kill Aisha. His conviction is not justice."

I walked away and he shouted from behind, "I hope you will give your Aisha the justice she deserved."

I didn't turn back and went off straight to the apartment I had rented. It was time to leave this place. It was, in fact, time for me to take to a sojourn so that I could put my past firmly behind me and move off to my carefree, reckless life.

My apartment had been broken in. Someone had entered, because the door was open. Surprisingly, nothing was stolen. There was an envelope with a USB in it, lying next to the television set.

There was a paper next to it. It said, "Call me if you want to do something about this – Aryan." There was a number below it.

The struggle is sometimes long, son, but the end has to be good winning over evil. Evil, however, destroys a lot before it gets what it deserves.

375

"Mom, why are some people murderers?"
"They are fanatics, son."
"Don't they feel the pain of the person they murder?"
"Psychopaths do not feel anyone else's pain,
They are driven by it."
"Do these people deserve to live, Mom?"
"They don't deserve to live, son.
They should be put to death just like a mad dog on the street."

I had a sinking feeling. I was done with the entire incident. I hadn't been able to eliminate Aisha out of my mind, but I was done with the entire incident. I had waited around for six whole months just focusing on the case. My life had been on a hold and all this while, I was just unable to get Aisha out of my mind.

I left the USB there and went off to pack my stuff. It was time I took off from India. I had to get out to forget about her and to kick-start my vagabond existence again. My bags took some time to pack. I got everything ready and was set. I dragged my luggage to the door and the house looked quite empty.

All this while, the USB was right there. It was on the shelf. I absolutely, completely did not want to watch that video. I had seen it through. It was time to leave this country if I had to preserve my sanity.

What if the video was just further proof that Bhim did it? It would help me sleep better. There was, however, the possibility that someone else did it. In which case, I would be completely at sea. Maybe, in that case, I could hand over the tape to the police and they would take care of it. Then again, why would that man give me the video? Maybe, this video was about something else entirely. It could be of some parallel issue which had nothing to do with this rape and murder.

I had a sinking feeling in my stomach. It was difficult to not see that video, especially when it was right there. I moved towards the TV set with slow steps, contemplating on every step that I took on whether I should go back. The TV set went on.

There was a man dressed in a politico's garb. There was another dressed in typical security uniform who was quite bulky. The bodyguard was pulling Aisha inside the house and she was shouting and shrieking. I still haven't figured out how they picked her up and why was she selected as a target for sexual abuse. I guess some explanations are not meant to come out and it didn't matter. She was stolen from me and that was all that mattered.

It was fuzzy and one could only make out the rapist's face once in a while. Most of the times, I just saw Aisha struggling and kicking. The house was quite equipped with a lot of showpieces. I still remember seeing a photo of a Hindu goddess mounted on the top of the wall. I guess she was on the wrong side right about then. There was an ongoing struggle and Aisha was kicking and pushing as much as she could, but the bodyguard had a strong grip. She knocked over one or two of the showpieces and the bodyguard slapped her almost unconscious. She was panting. Her face was wet because of the tears that were coming out from her eyes continuously. There was a hallway with a camera which led to the bedroom.

They had almost stripped her by the time they carried her to the room. She was shouting loud and clear for someone to save her. The room was not shut and the act was done in front of the bodyguard who disgustingly licked her while he was dragging and holding her against her will.

She was shouting loudly, "Leave me, please let me go. I beg you to let me go."

She was crying and somehow all that did was make them more brutal.

"My father only has me."

There was no respite. I was numb when I was watching the video. How could someone be so cruel? I just wanted to hold both of them by their necks and execute them with a scythe slowly. I hoped that they would go through pain.

She was violated beyond belief and ravaged. One could see the beastly look on the rapist's face and the dry, cold look of his bodyguard who did his share of violating her body. There was a woman who tried to interfere. The video didn't catch her well. The man in the white kurta seemed to hurl her to the wall, where she hit her head and was bleeding. No one attended to her and after a while, there was just a pool of blood in a corner. That part of the video went stagnant.

I couldn't make out anything except for the fact that the bodyguard kept going in and coming out. There were shouts and screams coming from within the bedroom. I could hear her shout, plead and beg. She first tried to save herself from the rape and then from the physical assault. This went on for half an hour, before I couldn't make out anything, except that after half an hour I saw some blood on the bodyguard's shirt. His boss came out and wiped his face. It was cold, almost as if he was used to it and Aisha was one of many victims.

The video went blank after that. I went numb. I had just seen the woman I was meant to be with raped. I felt as if I was being smothered. I stayed silent for a while and then screamed out loud. It felt as if something was piercing my stomach from inside and I was having difficulty breathing, I wanted to kill the man in the movie then and there, and if he were close to me, in a fit of rage, I might have.

I remember the day I watched the video. I wanted to do something to myself that day. But somehow I did not. I kept myself stable. I had heard of the weak legal system in India and the fact that they were ready and willing to pin the crime on whoever they could find, so I held myself back and did not go to a lawyer.

Who was this man? How did he get hold of Aisha? Where could I find him? What could I do about it even if I did find him? Could I turn him in to the cops? Would the legal system take care of it? What about Bhim? How the hell was a video of the entire incident shot? Why didn't it reach the police?

Yadav was right. Bhim did not do it. Maybe I was supposed to go back to Yadav and show him this. Would he be interested in bringing the truth out now?

There were a million thoughts crossing my head. A lot was said and discussed during Bhim's trial. Yadav had presented the definition of rape. He read out this section on rape in the Indian Penal Code

Section 375 of the Indian Penal Code.

Rape – A man is said to commit "rape" who, except in the case hereinafter excepted, has sexual intercourse with a woman under circumstances falling under any of the six following descriptions: Against her will, without her consent, and with her consent, when her consent has been obtained by putting her or any person in whom she is interested in fear of death or of hurt.

He then continued, "They forgot a clause. There is apparently an unsaid one which says that if you are strong and powerful in India, nothing will happen to you. You can rape, mutilate and degrade as many women as your heart desires. You just have to make sure you have the money to cover your ass when the police comes knocking at your door. If you are a politician, you won't even hear the knock. Bhim is a small man, hence the law got so far."

It didn't seem like the law was going to get very far. The man who was on the television screen seemed to be powerful at first impression.

In comparison, I was very small in the world order. In fact, I hardly knew anyone. No one was aware I existed. The only woman who knew that I was alive was just mutilated in the worst way possible and left lifeless by the men on the screen.

Once the rapist came out, there was little noise from inside. It fell silent. A rape and possible murder had just been committed. It was no big deal.

He looked at the bodyguard and said, "Can you check whether she's alive?"

The bodyguard bent to see if she was breathing. "She's not breathing."

He cleaned his face with a handkerchief and with no semblance of emotion in his voice said, "Throw her body on the streets so that it looks as if some animals from the road did this to her."

He pointed at the woman who was in a pool of blood after hitting the wall, "What do I do about the second one?"

"Leave her there. I want to stare at that one for a while. After all, we have a past. I'll take care of her, don't worry."

A question that kept on lingering in my head was who left the video outside my house and why didn't the concerned person leave it outside the police premises or something. A bigger question was whether I was going to do something about what I saw.

By definition, a psychopath is someone who is unaffected and cold. He is driven harder by someone's pain. They should be put to death quite akin to mad dogs...

Ek villain – there's one in every love story

"Why is there so much evil in this world, Mom?"
"Evil exists within all of us, son.
We are all fighting a constant battle against our evils
For a few, the battle is well lost
They cross over to the dark side
They justify everything that they do.
Hence, everything that happens to them also can't be questioned
The choices you make determine the man you are
The consequences of those actions will catch up with you sooner or later."

Ever wondered why evil exists? I have never been able to figure it out. I have asked so many people this question and got weird answers. Some say it exists so good can prevail over it. Some justify its existence on the Karmic theory. What is the karma of a child who is ravaged or killed when he is born? To this people answer it's your Karma of a previous life. Why would god not make someone suffer in this life for your deeds immediately? That just makes more sense than punishment for something that you are not aware you did.

I investigated about the man in the video. I took his photo off the video and showed it to a few people. Apparently, it didn't take much research. He was quite widely known and hated. But, my judgement of his power was right. He was a politician named Dayashankar Pandey. He was a political personality and a member of the Legislative Assembly in the state of Maharashtra, India. He had held key ministerial portfolios in the state at different times.

I wish Mr. Dayashankar Pandey was not born. Why didn't an accident happen to him at his birth? His mother could have had a miscarriage, his father could have killed him at birth or something more gruesome could have happened to him. But, I guess some people are born to cause pain and suffering in the world.

Revenge is the purest of all evils. In this case, however, it was clear that if I set out to seek revenge, the rest of my life was over. Mr. Pandey was a powerful man. There was a high possibility I would die in the process of killing him, without harming a hair on his head. There was also an outside possibility that I would kill him and his family would come after me with a vengeance. Given the power wielded by the family, they could do whatever they wanted.

I spent the next few days finding out about Pandey. I wanted to know who this man was. I met a few people who hated him and had somehow been affected by him. I got friendly with a few who told me about him. Maybe, if I found the right opportunity or information about him, I could find out the right way to get revenge from him.

He was a huge man who had everything in the world. He was big, bulky and had a huge moustache. His attire was quite political. Money, power, an obedient wife and yet somehow that wasn't enough. He had a weakness – young women. Lust was a major driver in his life and his power helped him get whatever and whoever he wanted. He was an animal in human form, greedy for money, flesh, et al.

He had risen from the grass root where he first worked for the party as a worker. He was quite talented in getting results using any means possible. He was an expert in manipulating systems and people and was willing to go to any extent to get them. He committed the crimes needed to climb the ladder of politics. Murders, and rapes were *'business as usual'*.

He would wear a kurta pyjama with a linen jacket over it. He was reckless with his speech, yet quite popular in his area since he gave people in his constituency enough money. His dialogues evoked anger among everyone, yet Mr. Pandey could not be touched.

He once said, "Rape is because women nowadays don't know how to dress up". When that evoked strong reactions, he refused to retract saying, "I was referring to the loss of our culture". Women protested outside his house and he apparently picked a couple of them out and told his guards to track them and get them to his house when they were alone.

India is a banana nation according to many, where the powerful rule and do whatever the hell they want. He could say whatever he wanted and do anything he desired. It was crazy that a man can have so much power and no accountability whatsoever. The entire Indian political scenario was full of such Pandeys. Clearly, democracy had worked exactly as the nation's founding fathers envisaged it would.

He married at an early age and got a wife who would be a good maid and stay at home managing his shit. She was a beautiful, meek woman named Nirmala. His wife was not allowed to have an opinion and was supposed to implicitly accept everything Pandey said or did. The whole world was not supposed to question, so how would his wife dare.

His wife had recently died. No one knew how. There were rumors about the fact that he himself might have murdered her. There was no proof, no case, no question raised. Pandey was inscrutable.

His family was not much known to the world. He never advertised them and I guess no one bothered to find out. His wife was a non-personality and no one knew or talked about his kids or family life.

The fodder he gave to the few journos who followed him around with his smart one-liners gave them enough to talk about and mock him. He did have a son who was quite low profile. He never presented himself in public. Apparently, he was estranged and absent from public life.

Aisha had come back to India for a short while only. She was supposed to be there for six months. She had to go there for her father who was alone in India. I don't really know how she ended up in Pandey's hands. There were a lot of pieces missing in the puzzle. But the net result was quite clear. Aisha had been Pandey's victim.

For a week, I found out whatever I could about Pandey. After a week, I decided to further my information and develop a plan of action. Maybe the man who had given me the videotape would suggest a further course of action. The only problem was I didn't know who gave me the tape.

I analyzed the contents of the USB again to get some clue as to who might have been able to reach the tape and who passed it on to me. All this was futile.

A week on, I had achieved nothing. I did not know what to do, who to go to and where to proceed. I had given up and realized the best option might be to pass the tape on to the cops. There was a high chance though that if I did it in person, Pandey would come after me. So, I decided to pass it over discreetly. It was probably useless but the only option that I had.

A letter came to my house that day by courier. It had my name on it and a number. The letter just said *'9833201234'*.

I gave a call on the number immediately. Someone picked up.

He immediately said, "I'm assuming you've got the tape. If you want to achieve true justice, meet me at The Oberoi hotel, Mumbai. Make sure you don't talk to anyone about anything."

There are two kinds of people in the world – evil ones who are bent to spoil society and life and the good who are society's only chance. People like me are on the sidelines – among the ones who didn't care. God tests us to the hilt. He puts us, the ones on the fringe, right in the front and we hardly have any choice in the matter.

I had two choices from here – ignore and forget everything, or make sure Pandey paid for the hell he put Aisha through. In my mind, however, I knew there was only one choice. There was no way for me to live any kind of a life without restoring the proverbial 'balance'. There are some they say who are born to lead and uproot the assumptions of the system – people meant to be a 'Che'. There are others like me who have no choice….

The choices you make determine the man you are, and the consequences of those actions will catch up with you sooner or later.

Something to die for

"I love you so much, son, that I would do anything for you."
"Will I experience that kind of love, Maa? Will I feel so much love for
someone that I will give my life up for her?"
"A person who hasn't found something to die for,
hasn't really loved.
When you love someone so much
That is when you have really lived."
"Have you found someone this close, Maa?"
"Yes, honey. You."

His name was Aryan. He had called me to this hi-fi hotel to have a conversation. Aryan was a tall, handsome man who was quite well-dressed. I was trying to figure out who he was and how he was related to Aisha, but no connection made sense except that he might have been an ex-flame or a one-sided lover. The latter seemed unlikely since he was quite handsome to not be able to charm Aisha, but you never know with these women. He could not have been her current lover, at least not in my head, because she clearly belonged to me before her death.

He was waiting for me in the majestic hotel's grand lobby. It was one of the best hotels I had seen in Bombay, bang opposite to the Queen's necklace.

Aryan was sitting in the coffee shop. I walked and sat down in front of him.

"Nice place."

He looked at me and immediately said, "I know. It's my treat here."

I looked at him with a bit of disgust, offended by the suggestion that I could not foot the bill, "I can pay as well, you know. I do have the money."

"Really. I thought you are just a vacationer."

I thought to myself, "How the hell did he know that about me?"

I snubbed him off saying, "I don't really have to tell you that. Now, do you have something you want to talk to me about?"

"Yes, I want you to kill the man who did this to Aisha."

I stared at him for five minutes. The first instinct that I got was that it was a comment made without thinking. But his face did not show any sign of a smile and the manner with which he had said that had a palpable calmness to it, which was quite eerie.

"I'm sorry. What do you want me to do?"

"I want you to kill the man who did this to Aisha," he said again, without hesitation.

I started to get up and go. The man in front of me was probably crazy. He was expressionless even while I was leaving.

Suddenly the waiter came up to the table.

He calmly told the waiter to get a Blue Label and a Chivas Regal on the rocks.

He had done his homework well. He knew the drink I had, my occupation and I would not be surprised if he knew the colour of my underwear.

I walked out nevertheless. I did not want to get into this dangerous conversation. Outside, there was a small paanwala with cigarettes on him, so I took a pack of smokes from him and lit up one.

"Don't have this. It will kill you," she said with a frown on her face. She looked beautiful even when she frowned. She had this amazing life on her face and this incredible belief that she could make me do anything she wanted.

"You are trying to make me a better person. That will kill me. My mother used to try that."

She said, "Okay. Keep having it."

I behaved like an adolescent child and continued to have the cigarette. She suddenly turned and snatched it from my mouth.

I felt the cigarette leaving my lips and felt the snap of her finger in front of my eyes.

"She didn't like you smoking, did she?" He took the cigarette from my lips.

I looked at him with a touch of sadness on my face, "No."

"You should come in. Your drink is getting warmer."

I looked at him for a while, took a deep breath and said, "Okay."

He smiled. When I was walking in the lobby towards the coffee shop, I had this sinking feeling that I was going to be complicit in his plan, even though I was petrified at the thought of what was just put in front of me on the table.

I sat down and said, "Who are you?"

"There are two rules. You will not ask me how I am related to Aisha or why I want to kill the man who did this to her. The other one is you will do as I say right till the end of this assignment."

"I am not your contract killer. I haven't even said yes yet."

He smiled. "You're almost done with that drink. Do you want one more?"

I looked at him and shrugged. "Why not?" I paused for a while as he ordered.

I took a look at the menu. The Oberoi could bankrupt me faster than international chains. It was a good thing Aryan was paying for it. As soon as the waiter left, I looked at him. "Why the hell are *you* not killing him?"

"I can't. The plan needs someone to shoot from a distance. I have extreme myopia which can be corrected only to a degree. I don't trust any of the contract killers because they tend to be part of a network which leaks its way back when a powerful man such as the one in question here is killed."

"Why can't we just hand over this evidence to the police?"

"Even if I send this video to the media and there is some hoopla about the case, there would be some outrage towards him. However, he will contest that the video was made to malign him. He has a lot of money. He can buy policemen, courts, everyone. He is no Bhim. He might even go to jail for a month. But after the outrage dies, he will be out. He will prove everything was an opposition manoeuvre. He will let the case go on, somehow destroy the video, kill everyone and anyone who can be possible evidence or who is associated with the video. He will get away for sure. He is a politician and a corrupt one. These people can't be touched in India."

"Right. How did you get the video?"

"Someone who was working for him managed to get the CCTV evidence before he destroyed it. You can think of it as an opposition manoeuvre." He smiled.

I looked at him and said, "I don't understand why he would do this to her."

"I hear you want to restore balance. You've seen the protests and the case progress. This is the only possible way to ensure justice is served."

"I am not strong enough to do this. I am a vagabond. Also, I don't know if we had that true love."

He looked at me and smiled.

"What?"

"You wouldn't have come back to this table or met her father if you didn't."

"Were you following me?"

He smiled and said, "Does it matter?"

"Both these things have an explanation," I said.

"I'm listening."

I looked at him, "I feel bad for the father and I was getting free drinks here."

"That would explain the speed then. Do you want another drink?"

"Yes."

"She had this wonderful zest for life, didn't she?"

"Yes."

"You guys have any proof that you were ever together. Any photos, messages exchanged, etc."

"No."

"Perfect"

"Listen, I'm not killing Mr. Pandey."

"You're hiding something from me. He pointed towards my heart."

"What?"

"You're hiding your pain and your love. You know that you feel hollow when you do not know your true purpose. The one person who affected you positively has been brutally assaulted like wild animals feeding on their prey. You want to find something to die for. After all, what is this life if not worth sacrificing it for someone else? They took her dreams, her hopes, her essence and her existence. You have to take theirs."

I was exasperated after listening to him. "You're convincing me to kill someone."

"Well, I am telling you to kill a wild animal who raided the body of someone who was probably the only one you ever loved."

I took a deep breath and flashes of Aisha and the gruesome video went through my head. "Let me think about it, okay."

He stared at me with piercing eyes, "Okay."

For a while, my head kept on oscillating between two thoughts. One, the fact that Aisha had been raped and murdered brutally and the legal system had collapsed around the criminal, so there was effectively no justice. That meant if there had to be someone who avenged the loss, it had to be me. On the flip side, I had a great life before meeting Aisha which I could continue with the pain of her death looking over my head. My life was pretty awesome and it was quite tempting to go back to the wasted, purposeless existence and roam the world while I was at it.

I sort of knew when I was going to meet Aryan that it had to do with something like this. I was going to be recruited for a murder. Yet, this was the last stage where if I took the call; there was absolutely no turning back.

It was late evening and the sky had a yellowish colour to it, the one just before nightfall. I was quite scared of the setting sun. I guess it was because it reminded me of my mortality. It was the worst time to take such a decision because between purpose or emptiness, nine times out of ten, you will tend towards the one which gives you a purpose.

So, I deferred my decision and went to a bar and got drunk. There were a few hot ladies out there, but I wasn't up to the task. I was lost in my own world.

I got out of the bar and it was quite dark outside. I had just got out on the Gateway of India side. It was a weeknight and except a few drunken poor guys on the street, there was no one else. Some locations in South Bombay can get quite lonely at night.

The Grand Taj Hotel was to my left and I was drifting by the wayside. The street lights were not working. I was quite drunk and the headlights from the odd vehicle that whizzed me by seemed like the sun had come down to earth.

After about an hour of me moping by the Arabian sea and listening to the sounds of the waves hitting the walls on the shore, I decided to sit my ass on the walls there.

I had almost made up my mind on what I was going to do. There was a pat on my back and a guy sat next to me handing me a beer.

I looked at him as he said, "This is like bunjee jumping, except once you get into the lift and go up there, there is no turning back. You *have* to jump. You can't look down and say you're not doing this."

"Dude, you've got to stop following me. I'm a recluse who works better when no one knows anything about him."

"Someone once said that a man who hasn't found something to die for isn't fit to live. I don't know who said it though."

He started laughing and I joined in after a while. In some time, we were laughing uncontrollably and sipped down our beers right to the last drop. I started to cry while laughing and he patted my back. I just couldn't stop. He hugged me.

"You know the toughest thing about losing her?" I started talking on my own.

"What?"

"The mind oscillates between the time I spent with her and the way she was killed. It's like there's this guilt that is accompanied with those memories, you know. The fact that she did not deserve it and no one is around to do anything about it. Just like I'm sure that no one was around when that bastard picked her and got her home. When someone you love is taken from you like that, the memory of that loss tends to overcome the memories of those moments that were so special. It's as if in one moment, Pandey wiped away an entire past."

He raised his drink to me. "Blood for blood, my man."

I raised my bottle as well and said, "Blood for blood."

Out of the blue, suddenly he said, "Martin Luther King."

"What?"

"It was Mr. King who said that."

I looked at him with a sad smile and managed a couple of laughs. We were drunk that night. It was ironic. I had a companion in my misery. It's quite difficult to picture if you haven't been in that situation. We were two drunk men staring at the blank sky, laughing and crying without much reason. Truth be said, there was no humour in our situation.

The night was destined to give way to the morning the next day, just as I was destined to bring justice to the memories of the only girl I have ever truly loved.

A man who hasn't found something to die for, hasn't really loved.

The mission begins

"I have lost focus, Maa. I just don't think anything is important
anymore. Do you think I'll do anything great in my life?"
"You will find focus when you least expect it.
If it's meant to be, he will test you when you least expect it.
How you respond do that test
Will define who you are and what you are meant to be."

"Death they say is only the beginning."

"We'll soon find out, you know. We are on an accelerated mission towards our death," I said, sadly.

"We don't have to sacrifice ourselves. We're out to execute, not be executed," Aryan said confidently.

"You're certain we won't get caught!" I was bowled over by his confidence.

"We will have to undergo training for that."

"Who will help us?"

"There is this ex-Major, Mr. Rai Bahadur Singh from the Indian Army. He will help us with what we want."

"Why will he help us?"

"He helps the cause of justice."

"How did you find out about him?"

"There were some vigilante acts a couple of years back in the city. A few criminals, rapists, murderers were killed. There were a couple of politicians who were also killed in this process. These acts were done with amazing level of precision. I was involved in some youth wing of this activist group. We started cheering, this unknown man. Somehow, I think the Major wanted me to reach out to him. Some person hinted who this vigilante was to me. Turned out, the acts were performed by multiple men who were trained by him. I reached out to the Major who had no hesitation to talk about what he was doing. It seemed as if he knew everything about me, my childhood. These guys are very resourceful."

"He doesn't believe in the legal system in place."

"The Indian legal system is funny that way. It is effective against the poor criminal but when it comes to a criminal who is a politico or for that manner anyone with money, there are so many loopholes in the system that he gets away. That's where vigilantes like you and me come in."

"Yeah. Batman and Robin."

He stared at me smiling. "Yeah, and this time, for a change, Robin is taking the shot."

"I think that's because the Dark Knight is losing his touch."

He looked at me, tongue rolled up. "Why so serious, son?"

"Anyway, we talked about a variety of issues including what he was doing currently. It turns out he was helping random youths who were wronged to get justice the only way possible in this country."

The Major was staying in a village near Mumbai, named Murud. It was around 165 kms from the city. A sleepy village, it was known mainly for the Murud-Janjira fort at the palace of the Nawab. It was a village blessed with natural beauty and known for the sea food preparations. The population was on the lower side and it was a silent place, which had historically never been in the spotlight for anything. It was an on and off tourist destination. People didn't really care about what was happening around them. It was the perfect hideout for a Major, who was into training potential superheroes.

We reached the village and asked for his address. He lived in what was a mansion large enough to accommodate a hundred people at least. It was designed in the Victorian Gothic style and was probably a pre-independence structure made with the help of the British, now being used as Wayne Manor for India's Bruce Waynes. It seemed like something straight out of a movie.

We were asked to sit down in the waiting area and a butler brought tea and biscuits for us. After a while, a sixty-plus-year-old man came up to us. Aryan immediately saluted the man. He then shook his hands.

The man was sixty-plus but one could be easily mistaken into believing that he was forty-five, or worst case, fifty. He was amazingly fit. He was smoking a cigar and wore a cap on his head. The man had class a.k.a. Robert De Niro or an Anthony Hopkins.

He scanned me from top to bottom and then looked at Aryan. "This is the man you got for the mission, eh?

"Yes, sir."

"I have my doubts, son."

"We are at your mercy, sir."

He sighed, patted Aryan's back and then looked at me. "What's your name?"

"Dhruv."

"That means prince, doesn't it?"

"Yeah, I guess it does."

"The prince is about to commit a sin."

"I guess so, sir."

"You loved her."

"Yes sir."

"You would kill for her."

"Yes sir."

"You would die for her."

"Yes sir."

"Then let's get you ready for the kill, son."

"Yes sir."

He patted me on the back and started to sip his tea. He started talking about the degradation of the moral fibre in the country. He did not discuss Aisha's murder, his past and we refrained from touching those topics as well.

At the end of the conversation, he looked at me and said, "Your pain is your biggest weapon, son. If you feel for her, that has to come out. We start training for the kill tomorrow, but only if you truly believe you loved the one you're avenging so much that it hurts when you think of her. I will give you a night to think. If you still want to go ahead with it, we will continue tomorrow. If you don't, there will be a vehicle to drop you back to Mumbai and then you can head back to wherever you come from."

"Sir, is that the only criteria? Don't you want to know about my physical fitness, my weight, vision etc?"

"Son, you are not wearing glasses. You seem to be of a good build. The only other criteria you have to satisfy is this one. By the way," he pointed to Aryan, "this one could have killed the target himself, but he did not because of his vision. He is quite myopic."

I flatly asked Major Singh, "Sir, why does he want to kill Mr. Pandey? Was he in love with Aisha as well?"

Major Singh looked at me and gave a faint smile. "Son, his motive was never revealed to me. I did not ask his motive and will not ask you yours. I judge people straight up and then trust that they are doing the right thing. I then train them for that one perfect shot so that they can spend the rest of their lives in peace without the thirst for vengeance consuming them."

"Right, sir."

"So you have tonight for deliberation, son. Have a good night sleep. The butler will take your order for dinner. You have the option of eating in the room or joining me for dinner at 9 p.m. at the table."

"I'd rather have dinner with you, sir."

"Right. Then I'll see you gentlemen at dinner."

I was guided to my room along with Aryan. We had separate rooms. It was like checking into the Taj, only better. The rooms were as large as they could be. There was bare minimum furniture, but the interiors were brilliant. The man definitely had class.

I didn't even need to think through whether I was going back this time. It was now just a question of getting started.

How you respond to the test God puts you through will define who you are and what you are meant to be

One more round

"Mom, I am tired of studying. It's so difficult. I don't want to do this."
"Son, you have to work hard to be successful in what you want to do
Life gives you limited opportunities
You have to struggle to make sure you come good
Just keep telling yourself that you can last for one more round. Just one
more round."

The training was set to begin. I was asked to get up at six in the morning. It was the first time someone had asked me to get up at that time.

The Major's house was huge. There was a lawn in front of the house which was at least about five hundred metres in radius. It was replete with greenery.

I reached the spot right at the time mentioned and was more than half sleepy.

The Major looked at me, "You don't look ready to kill someone, son."

I stared at him with half opened eyes. With him was Aryan who was almost fully awake.

Aryan looked at me and said, "Rise and shine, sunshine."

I was able to comprehend half of what was being said to me. The words were all garbled. It was like I was intoxicated. I was almost half asleep when a splash of extremely cold water came straight at my face.

It felt as if my face was numb. My face started shivering and my teeth were rattling. I stared at both of them with an intention to start my murders from here.

The Major looked at me and said, "Are you awake now? Are you ready to kill someone?"

With a voice which barely came out of me, I said, "Can I bail out? This is the toughest thing I have ever done."

Aryan looked at the Major who asked him, "He thinks this is tough. You think this man can kill someone?"

The Major pretended not to listen to Aryan and raised his voice, "Do you not regret that Aisha was raped? Do you not want to avenge her? Do you want to live this life as a worthless creature who could not give justice to the one he loved?"

I slumped down to the grass. The Major continued, "People like you deserve to have this come upon you. You should go home and continue your futile existence. Aisha deserved what she got and Pandey will get many more like her."

I wasn't responsive. He started to turn away with Aryan, "You're right, Aryan. He can't kill anyone. Let him go back."

I couldn't move for a while. I closed my eyes and flashes of Aisha came by. They say mental strength can overcome any and every physical limitation that the body may have.

A few tears came uninvited in my eyes, and I managed to get up. The Major did not look behind, but Aryan did. He kept his hand on the Major's shoulder. The Major turned and looked at me, all awake with slightly moist eyes, but mostly ready.

"Give me five rounds of this lawn, Dhruv."

I started to run with the Major and Aryan looking at me. After a round, Aryan started to run as well.

I turned back and looked at him, "Why the hell are you running?"

He smiled back at me. "I also have to train. I'm going to be there with you."

"Who's taking the shot? Me or you."

He smiled and looked at me, "Do you want to take it?"

I looked up and then at him, "Yes, I want to be the one to kill him."

I almost collapsed at the end of the third round. I looked at the Major to see if he approves of three rounds and if I could take the remaining after a while. His eyes were unrelenting. I mustered the courage to run the last two rounds. Aryan was quite fresh as he raced through the lawns sprinting. Maybe, he was supposed to be the one who pulled the trigger. If his eyesight had been normal, he would have been the Major's first choice to kill Pandey.

I was panting, sweating and out of all energy when Aryan caught up with me and lowered his pace, "Do you remember her a lot?"

I looked at him, "Yes."

"What was your favorite memory of her?"

"She was full of this energy, you know. I was futile and useless to most. Yet, she hardly judged me and listened to me. After my mother, she was the only person who I connected with. She was perfect in so many ways."

I didn't realize while I was talking that I had completed my fourth and was midway on my fifth. I made it to the end point and Aryan was smiling.

The Major came up to me and patted me on my back. "Well done!" He smiled and looked at Aryan who smiled back.

He looked at me and said, "I see potential in you, son. You have been wronged and I believe that you will do anything it takes to get revenge."

The Major gave me a bottle of water and looked at me and said, "You now have to do fifty sit-ups and fifty push-ups."

"I can't," I said.

"Oh, but you can."

Aryan took the ground to start push-ups. The Major looked at me and I was on the ground reluctantly. Aryan went like a rocket, while I was quite slow. I did twenty and collapsed on the ground.

Aryan took a break and looked at me. "Go slow. Don't tell your body you're tired. Take it one by one."

I somehow managed to finish thirty push-ups out of the fifty and fell flat on the floor. I was completely devoid of energy and enthusiasm by then.

The Major exhorted loudly, "Get up, son! We have twenty more to go."

I looked at him with coy eyes, "Am I training for a murder or the Indian Olympics?"

He replied almost instantly, "There ain't much difference in the training for both. Both vocations need fit youngsters. Ever heard of an old, tired man committing murder?"

I replied immediately, "Pandey."

After a five minute hiatus on the floor, I resumed the push-ups. My body was in extreme pain, but I guess I had to be experiencing more pain in my mind for me to be able to complete the outrageous targets set by the tyrannical Major.

I was panting profusely and had no feeling left in my arms. I looked at the Major, who seemed to care little about me. Aryan went inside for a glass of water which incidentally I was not allowed to drink.

Aryan came back and offered me a couple of sips, even though the Major objected. As soon as I finished those precious sips, the Major thundered, "Let's do a hundred pull ups."

I looked at the Major and said, "Sir, with all due respect, are you training me to kill or planning to kill me because quite frankly, I might die of fatigue."

The Major did not listen to my objections and took me to a place where a steel bar was placed between two trees. He looked at me and told me, "Go for it!"

I sighed and with very little energy jumped to grab the handle. The bar was at least three feet above me. I started the pull-ups with every little bit of energy that I could muster.

I don't know how many I could complete. I just remember falling on the floor and my head hitting the ground. I was unconscious for quite a while.

She looked like a small child smiling in front of her father. I was also there. I didn't recognize the child. She was very pretty and looked so innocent.

Her father called her out to, "Aisha."

I was watching all this from a distance. She ran to her father when called and was smiling all the way. Her smile was haunting. Suddenly, a man started to pull her away from her father. She was crying. Aisha was crying. I couldn't bear to hear her cry. I wanted to do something. I wanted to kill that man and make sure Aisha stopped crying. I rushed to her father to help him. I wanted to save her. How can anyone make such a beautiful child cry? I just wasn't able to reach out on time.

"Aisha…Aisha…."

All I could hear were some sobs and her name.

Aryan shook me and I woke up to see his face staring at me. I had moist eyes and was breathing heavily.

"She's haunting you in your dreams, man. You've got to focus on killing him even in your dreams."

I looked at Aryan and was silent for a while. I had no idea how to respond to anything. I took a deep breath and finally spoke up, "How long have I been out?"

"Seven-eight hours. Your body had been stretched to its limits."

I looked zoned out even now, so he said encouragingly, "Here, have a cup of coffee. You could use it."

I looked at him and was in a daze, "Yeah, I could use it."

The first day of training took a toll on my body. My body was in immense pain as the muscles had never been stretched so much. I somehow managed to close my eyes in the night and fell into a sound sleep.

I was woken up early morning and dragged to the grounds once again. The Major was waiting for me. I was half asleep yet again.

The Major thundered, "You have to do seven rounds today."

I did not waste any energy trying to object and started to run. Surprisingly though, it was a tad bit easier than the previous day. I guess my muscles had gotten slightly less tighter by the previous day's run.

Nevertheless, after five rounds, I paused and sat down. The Major started to come towards me. I waited until he came close and before he could reach me, I got up and started to run again. He smiled and looked at me and then turned to Aryan, "It's like training a small boy who's trying to act smart."

Aryan laughed and the Major smiled. The stark reality of what awaited us was quite obvious and the lighter moments promised to be lesser as time went by. Life was just about to get tougher by the instant and the mission that we had set to achieve was fast approaching.

The Major thundered at the end of my sixth, "One more round, son. Just one more round…."

Life gives you limited opportunities, son. You have to struggle to come good on them. Just keep telling yourself that you can last for one more round. Just one more round.

Ready for the kill

"Mom, I am not strong enough to take care of you."
"You are, son. You take good care of me."
"No, I don't earn for you, I see you working hard all day and I can't do
anything about it."
"You're my purpose, son
I wouldn't have survived without you
We all need that something to carry on
You are that something for me, my entire life."

The trouble will not be in committing the murder. It will be in getting away with it. The training being imparted by the Major had multiple facets to it, one of them being to escape after the act. He was first trying to get me fit and ready. I was then to go through training on a shooting post and later, I was to enact the escape for which he had designed a simulation of his own. He was, according to Aryan, designing the perfect weapon to kill Pandey.

"It's all about the temperament. You will have to learn to be cool and yet focused in all situations. That is the primary motive of this training. It is to hone your reaction to situations and render you more like a robot who responds sequentially and does the processes needed with utmost precision."

After a week of rigorous physical training, my muscles had eased up. On the eighth day, I got up quite early in the morning myself and started the rounds before the Major came in. I completed ten rounds with ease post which I went for the push-ups without getting goaded into it.

Aryan looked at the Major and said, "He's ready."

The Major smiled, "Yes, I think we should have him training on guns now."

Aryan had a tear in his eye, "Our little bird is ready to fly."

The Major smiled ever so slightly. "Let's see how he performs with a gun in his hand."

He had a shooting range of sort. There was a target which was quite the usual one – the receding circles with the center in full sight. The goal was to hit the center as close as possible. I was handed a German rifle, a precision GmBH, and I held it up giving a pose quite akin to Antonio Banderas in one of those Mexican movies.

The Major smiled. I took my aim at the target and shot. There was a sound and I assumed the bullet had been shot. I experienced some recoil and the gun fell off my hands.

I looked at the Major, "What did I hit?"

The Major smiled and did not respond to my question. I looked at Aryan with quizzical eyes, hoping that he would answer my question.

Aryan frowned a bit, took a sigh and said, "You forgot to turn the safety off. There was no shot."

I looked at him in surprise, refusing to acknowledge that he may be correct. Then I smiled to avoid any embarrassment and still be their number one hitman choice and said with some confidence, "That's okay."

The Major smiled and said, "Try again. That's a classic rookie mistake. This time focus on the target, forget the style, take the safety off and try and anticipate some recoil so that you are stable after the shot. Also, don't forget to turn the silencer on. We don't want the gun to make any noise right from the start."

I took a deep breath and picked the gun up again. I calmed my nerves down, took the safety off and made sure that my footing was right. There was mud beneath my feet, so there were good chances of slipping. I made some sort of a depression on the ground and pushed my foot hard against it.

Both Aryan and the Major were observing closely. This was it. It was my first maiden shot with a gun. I had not ever participated in shooting ranges or any other activity of this sort. I focused on the target and pressed the trigger after giving myself time to point it in the right direction.

This time I knew that the gun did fire. There were four concentric circles with reducing radii. I was supposed the hit the center of the innermost and instead, I hit the edge of the second circle.

The Major looked at me and said, "Not bad. Try again. This time try to hit the first circle. Aim not for the center, but for the first circle."

I loaded the gun again and tried to focus, this time keeping my eye on the first circle giving myself some margin of error. I took a deep breath again and pulled the trigger. Bam.

After the shot, I checked to see how close I'd got. I had actually done worse than the first shot. This one had gone between the second innermost and the third.

I looked down and rubbed my eyes. Clearly, I wasn't that great at it. My eyes started to water and I realized that I had strained them quite a bit in taking these shots and yet ended up nowhere close to Pandey's head. I was probably going to hit him on his arm if I shot at this rate and he would get me shot in my head point blank range after a while after torturing me to hell, that is.

"You need to keep going," said the Major, "I have at least 30 bullets to waste for today's training."

"They will be a waste since I don't know what I'm doing. There must be some form or technique involved in this. Tell me what I am doing wrong."

"Your hands are trembling. Your head isn't completely stable. Your attention is not there 100 %."

"Hmmm…So what do I do now?"

"Well, you need to calm yourself down and work on these aspects. The first thing is to build your focus. You need to forget about everything around you. Try and throw any thought that you may have while you are taking the shot. You should be able to hear yourself breathe with your senses on high alert. Feel your muscles taking the shot and do not press the trigger unless the target looks bigger to you than it actually is. Make sure that you do not fall back even a centimeter because of recoil. Feel the movement in your hands and command them to stop shaking."

I listened intently to the Major. He was quite calm when he was talking about these things. Somehow, I could sense in his voice that he was not worried about me picking up on shooting as he was the day I could not complete his fitness regime. I guess for him, that was the major cut-off and this was just a time-bound process that was bound to yield results.

I let myself loose for a while and tried to meditate. I started to focus on my thoughts and my brain started to push them away. I could feel them slowing down and my head getting a lot lighter.

I turned my head to the target and walked towards it, this time with a lot more composure than the first two trials. I took the gun in my hands and felt them trembling. I focused on them till the shaking went down. In the earlier two shots, I had track of where Aryan and the Major were. In this attempt, they somehow weren't around in my head and my visibility. I focused on the target and started to notice the curvature of the circle with much more detail. There was a pen stain on the target right near the center, one that I had not noticed earlier. I felt the target to be much nearer than it actually was.

It was much smoother this time when I pressed the trigger and though it did not hit the center, the shot went right within the first circle.

"You need focus, you know."

"I don't know if I am a man who can develop that, Aisha. I'm more the superficial, lacks any sort of depth kinda person."

"Nah, you're just not motivated yet."

"Yup, I guess so. My mother recited the Mahabharata to me. She talked about the incident where Arjuna is looking at the eye of the fish and setting target. Apparently, he didn't see anything else. How does one get that kind of focus?"

She smiled, "You haven't found your purpose yet."

The Major smiled and I looked at him, "Not quite on target, is it?"

"No. It did not hit the centre. It was some distance away from it. You'll get there."

Aryan smiled as well and clapped his hands a bit. He wasn't close to as good at hiding his emotions as the Major. "Our perfect weapon is getting ready and Pandey's countdown has begun."

The Major had thirty shots for me that day. I took them one by one and he generated a sort of a report card which summarized my performance.

Day One

Target: 1
Circle I: 24
Circle II: 4
Circle III: 1

That report card was handed over to me and he said, "Benchmark yourself against the past day. There has to be continuous improvement."

"What percentage success implies I'm ready?"

The Major smiled, "You will know when you are ready."

I was sure I would never know. Clearly, he was the trainer and had better judgment than me, so I felt the dialogue to be a bit arbitrary, but let it go.

The training continued daily with the fitness regime at the start and the shots after that. I had a strict diet regime as well and it truly felt like I was in the army. The Major ran a tough academy for me.

It was day 7 and my report card read thus:

Day 7

Target: 7
Circle I: 20
Circle II: 2
Circle III: 0

I took the report card to Major, "I think I'm ready."

The Major looked at me, "Okay. Then we stop tomorrow."

I was shocked at his instantaneous response and felt a bit nervous, "No, no. Let me try more."

The Major patted my back and said, "Your choice, son."

The training continued and I started to focus harder. I was clearly not ready.

After about a week, my report card was as follows

Day 14

Target: 19
Circle I: 11
Circle II: 0
Circle III: 0

I mustered the courage and walked up to the Major. "I am ready, however I would like to gradually shut down the training and not instantly."

The Major nodded his head in agreement, "Done."

Aryan smiled and walked towards me, "Ready for Mr. Pandey?"

"I'm ready for the kill, for that one shot which will make or break his head."

Aryan called me for a drink. We went into the Major's bungalow and headed to his bar. Teak wood and a Victorianesque architecture made the bar look regal. I sat down on the chair and Aryan went behind the bar. He poured two Scotch whiskeys in a glass and put a lot of ice in both the glasses.

Aryan sat down on the barman chair and smiled. He raised his glass and said, "Cheers."

I smiled too. "Cheers."

He then asked, "You ever thought you would be prepared and fit to go through this training?"

I sipped down the whiskey instantly as if it were a shot offered to me. It felt a bit lighter while the whiskey seeped through my body. I could almost feel it relaxing my muscles. I took a deep breath and looked at him. I somehow managed a smile and said, "No, I did not."

He looked at me, "You're doing great."

"I guess so. The trick, however, is that practice tests are never as difficult as the real one."

"No, they are not."

He offered me another drink which I gulped down again.

"Slow down, mate."

"What do you think I should focus on that day?"

"I don't know, because truth be told, I'm not an expert on this either. I guess the few thoughts that you should allow yourself to have should be around Aisha because I've seen that increase your focus and determination to get it right."

"I can easily imagine the repercussions if I do not get the shot right. What happens if I do? What do I live for then? I will have lost my purpose."

"That's the problem a lot of us face after we reach the goal, mate. We do not know what to do after we get there. There's nothing much to accomplish after that."

"So, you don't have any suggestions."

"I have one."

"What?"

"You need to focus on getting it right. The question of what happens after that can be answered later."

I stared at him for a while sipping my fourth peg. This time, I did not gulp it down. "Right."

I was a bit high with my thoughts going helter-skelter. Whenever my head strolled back to the conversations I had with Aisha, there were so many similarities in how she and my Maa thought. Maybe, the nice people in my life were meant to die, or alternatively, I was so damaged with nothing to lose that I was brought into Aisha's life knowing that I would take revenge for the wrong done on her. After all, there has to be someone to maintain the balance. Given the odds in this case, it had to be someone like me with nothing to lose and no one to cry for him.

We all need that something to carry on. You are that something for me, my entire life.

How to get away
with murder

"How does one become a superhero, Maa?"
She smiled and puffed her cheeks, "By fighting for justice."
"Yes. I don't think I have it in me, though."
"There is a way to become a hero, son
You see, it is important to be just in your head first
You may seek justice from the world
First you need to find it within yourself."

The Major was happy that I was ready. Aryan had trained beside me as well.

Early morning the next day, Aryan was already in the garden training and the Major was counting his push-ups. I walked up to the two and asked him, "What has he been practicing for?"

The Major replied, "He's going to be there with you against my advice. I'm training him to escape."

"Why is he coming along?"

"Against my better judgement, he wants to. You better ask him. He will, however, have a better chance of escaping this than you if things go wrong."

"You're telling me I have a small chance of escaping if I go wrong."

"Yes."

The Major's honesty was quite unnerving at times. Sometimes, I wished there was someone more diplomatic training me, but I guess there was no way I could have trusted him if he were not so out there. It was, perhaps, better that the Major was who he was.

"Don't I have to be trained to escape as well? I would like to come out of this alive."

The Major looked at me and smiled. "I wouldn't mind that as well."

I shrugged and took a deep breath. "So, shouldn't I be training for the escape as well?"

"Yes, yes of course. I have to train you to escape as well. Give me fifty push-ups."

I looked at him and said, "I've been doing that for a long time now. I just want to train for the escape."

He gave me a stern look and thundered, "I won't repeat again, son. Give me fifty now."

I wasn't shaken up by his voice, but to avoid the boredom of arguing with the Major, I quietly acceded to his request and gave him fifty push-ups.

I finished the push-ups without much complaint or pain. Before I did, Aryan was up and erect waiting for me. I got up and looked at the Major, "What now?"

"You will have to jump off the window on the first floor with a rope tied to something. When you get down, you have to set fire to the rope so that you don't leave any trace behind," he said.

"So, do we have to jump off the first floor with a rope now?"

"Yes. That will be the start. From tomorrow, you will train off the terrace."

The trick when you are planning to kill someone is to know how to get away. The sight of blood should not deter you for a second so that you can plan your escape instantly. The kill has to be smooth, the movement synchronized according to plan up to the last instant and there has to be no emotion involved. There's no space for anger, remorse, empathy. All evidence needs to be cleaned up and an escape plan which ensures nothing gets left behind including the murderer.

"Jump," thundered the Major.

I looked at him and shook my head. I wasn't going to jump off the first floor with a rope. No one told me I needed to be Spiderman.

"Hold the rope, initially balance against the walls and slide down the rope. Be quick when you are sliding down and be careful that you don't leave the rope behind."

"Doesn't the remnant rope become evidence that gets left behind?"

"That rope is made of fine count cotton yarn which will burn without leaving behind residue. The fire will terminate at the end of a non-combustible support."

I looked at the Major and said, "How many times have you done this?"

The Major said in a commanding voice, "Enough. Now jump!"

I took a deep breath and jumped off the ledge. The ground below was bare and was at least thirty feet away. If I slipped from the rope, I was destined to hit the hard surface and would probably end up with no limbs. I was slow at the start and clung on to the rope as hard as I could. I then realized that I wasn't very bad at it, so loosened my grip and slipped a bit. My speed at the end was good. I touched the ground and shouted, "Major, how good was I?"

He shouted, "Slow. You took three-and-a-half minutes. You are supposed to take less than a minute."

"Aryan!" he looked at him and shouted.

Right after me, Aryan got ready to go down. He quickly took the rope from the Major's hand and shot down almost instantaneously. He was rapid. It was like he was in the Olympics. Except his vision, Aryan was definitely the best person for this job.

Aryan looked at me when he touched the ground. It was a condescending, *'I am better than you'* look. I've had people give me that look before. The trouble was that they were all better than me.

The Major shouted, "Slow. You took a minute and five seconds."

I stared at the Major with my mouth open in surprise. He thought Aryan was slow. I was a snail in comparison.

Aryan looked at me and patted my back, "We need to improve our timing if we want to get out of there without being caught."

We practiced the rope for multiple times. In our trials, I lost control once and fell right to ground with a thud. I was lucky that happened from five feet only.

I looked at Aryan. "We need to be really good at this, don't we?"

"Yes."

"What's your vision? You are otherwise perfect for the job."

"It's 6/12, even with glasses. I suffer from atrophy. I might need a corneal replacement once I'm old."

"Why the hell would you want to come and risk yourself? I can do the job."

"I wanted to do this job myself. But, given my circumstance, it passed on to you. I at least want the privilege of being there."

"How did the Major allow this? He would never allow anything to risk or complicate the mission."

"I did not give him a choice in the matter. This job will involve hours of waiting patiently. I believe I should be there to make sure you keep your focus and composure intact. We argued for hours at end, but he gave in, and here I am, all set to kill Pandey."

"I don't understand your motive."

"When the time is right, I will tell you."

I tried to get a bit cocky, "I think the right time has come."

"I am a man set on killing evil men. I'm Batman."

I smiled and patted him on his back. "Well technically, I am pressing the trigger and you are on the side. You are a sidekick…more like Robin. I am the Dark Knight."

Aryan smiled back. "The joker awaits."

The Major was silently watching the camaraderie at a distance. After a while, he approached us. "Let's get on the job if you guys are done idling away your time."

We got back to climbing down the rope. Every time we got down, we realized we were saving a fraction of a second more than the last. By the end of the training, we were down in about a minute flat.

It was quite difficult, however, when the height was increased. He took us to the terrace. When I looked down, I felt a bit dizzy. The Major, however, didn't give me much time to get ready. He had us on the rope and again started timing us. To be fair, given the extra height, he gave us a minute more in terms of a target. We got quite close and quite good at it.

On one of these trials, I accidently swung a bit and had to use my leg to push away from the wall a tad bit. I made a little bit of sound.

The Major immediately said, "You need to go down without any sound. No one should get alerted by your movements."

"Right."

We practiced a few more times to make sure we were doing it right. At the end of it, the Major asked us to burn the rope. We lit fire to the rope and it burned away. There was absolutely nothing left behind. The rope was gone as if it was never there."

"What about the location? What if they come to know?"

"They won't. There are five buildings in that area. The shot could come from anywhere. Also, you need to realize that the protection Pandey has is at best mediocre policemen. You will be in a flat housed by a reputed military professional. Even if they want to, they can't break into the house without prior warrants. The next day, a servant will come to the house and clean any and everything that is left behind."

I looked at the Major with awe. "You've planned this to the utmost detail, haven't you? To do all this homework, there has to be motive. What the hell is the motive for you guys? You clearly know why I'm doing this."

The Major looked into my eyes and without blinking said, "My only motive is to rid this country, that I promised to defend, of people like Pandey who don't deserve to exist here."

The Major said this and started to walk away. Aryan went off with him. I shouted loudly from behind, "That's bullshit and you guys know it."

The Major did not turn. Aryan did. He smiled and shouted back, "You better get some sleep. Batman begins very soon."

I had come a long way and surpassed my expectations. I still had some fears to overcome though. The fate of the mission however, literally rested on a rope and on me. Practice sessions apart, there was one question lingering in my head. Would I truly deliver when the moment demanded that from me?

You may seek justice from the world. First, you need to find it within yourself.

Plan of the perfect kill

"Why do men kill each other, Maa?"
"Some men kill for pleasure
Some kill for revenge
But it isn't right to take a life.
That is best left to God."
"Soldiers do it to defend us, Maa. People sometimes take lives to
avenge the wrong. Are all of them wrong?"
"Sometimes son a life is taken not to avenge the one lost
But to protect further loss of innocent lives."

I woke up feeling quite tired. It had been days of training and the physical exhaustion had taken quite a bit out of me. I had been through military training and given my wayward background and behaviour, it was quite ironic that I ended up doing all that I had.

I walked out early morning to the ground again. There was no one there that day. It was surprising. For about two months now, I had constantly been under pressure from the Major to never be late, and today, both the Major and Aryan had been tardy. This was an interesting turn of events.

I was smiling smugly to myself for a while. I waited there for fifteen minutes, wondering how long it was going to take them.

After a long wait, I figured out something was wrong. I made my way towards the Major's house and headed towards the living room.

Both the Major and Aryan were quietly sipping their tea. I looked at them with a bit of surprise and asked, "Aren't we training today?"

Aryan smiled and said, "Nope. Training's done."

I took a deep breath. That statement meant a lot of things. It meant they believed I was set to kill. It also implied the dreaded day was quite near now.

The Major looked at me and said, "You are now the perfect weapon. There's nothing more I can teach you. Dayashankar's time has come."

I sat down besides the two of them. They poured me a cup of tea. The Major carefully pulled out a brand new Gernam GmBH rifle. It was quite akin to the one that I practiced on. He handed it to me.

"It's a brand new rifle. You have practiced on a similar one. This one just needs to be tested with a few shots, which I trust you will do."

I took a sip and looked at the Major. "Now what? When have you planned the mission?"

"In a week's time."

"Why do we want to wait for a week?"

"Even though you've been trained, we need to do some reconnaissance of the area where we plan to carry out the act. We will take you to the place. You have to absorb the place, take in all the elements and the surroundings. Each and every aspect of the place should be in your memory."

"Won't people get suspicious?"

"You will be disguised every time you go there. Pandey's office is located in the building named Trilok. You have to look for a building called Elegance towers. You will be making the shot from there. The building is not very well guarded and has a wall on the opposite side which is quite scalable. You will be making the shot from the fifth floor of that building. Watch the happenings around the area quite closely.

There is a restaurant around that area, so sit yourself down there and order something while taking a look at how close cars are parked to the pavement and the exact interval people take to get from the car to the building.

"You have to measure the steps it takes from the pavement to the building, so first get an idea of where cars are parked and then walk towards the building from the spot that you mark. Walk straight without any interruptions and measure the steps one takes to get to the building. Mark the angles of the shot. Take a look at people around to get a sense of how busy the street is. It takes at least ten seconds before the man who is shot collapses and the bullet starts to have an effect. If the street is busy, there won't be many others who react to the shot. That will be the time you take to reach for the rope. The first reaction of the body guards will be to take him and put him down on the floor. One of them could possibly rush to figure out the perpetrator. By the time he moves, you should be on the rope. You have to make sure that people around don't have the time to react."

"Okay."

The spot of the kill was in a lane. It was a crowded place. The first time, I went there with a fake moustache and goggles looking like a '70 superstar. A lot of hustle and bustle around meant there was time to escape after the act.

The Major added, "I have also planned a procession to pass through at that time which I'll be leading. I will time it to hit that area exactly at the time of the shot. The idea is to create as much disturbance around as possible. The bodyguard should not get any idea of where the shot came from. I'll try and initiate a ruckus in the most discreet way possible and try and divert any attention towards the building."

There was a bookstore, a general store and a medical store among the organized mom and pop stores. The stores weren't too much of a problem. The issue was with the hawkers in the lane. It was like a mini Walmart broken into small pieces and instead of the huge callouts in Walmart which shout out the price, actual men were shouting at the top of their voices. Multiple vendors were fighting for the same customer. All I noticed was all of them were losing.

Trilok was easily identifiable. It was quite posh and had a glass exterior with svelte offices that were visible from outside. I decided to get into the building. Every floor had two offices and there was no sound coming out of anywhere. It was incredible. You couldn't hear the hawkers or anything else. The glass was extremely sound proof.

Elegance was right next to it. There was nothing special about that building. It was quite dilapidated and run down. Apparently, the building was due to be razed in a week or two. The residents of the building were shifted to allow for the reconstruction.

The area right in front of the gate of Trilok was quite clear with watchmen getting hawkers to steer clear. I kept a watch on the cars that were approaching. Most of the drivers left the guests right next to the gate of the building. The guests would then walk for about a metre-and-a-half before there was a roof above their head.

I sat down at the restaurant bang opposite Trilok. I took a paper and starting doing some work. Based on Pandey's age and build, he would probably walk at 3km/hour. To cover one-and-a-half-metre, he would take around 3 seconds to reach safety. Add to that a couple of seconds for him to get out of the car. The muzzle velocity of the bullet is about 400 ft/second. The approximate distance from the flat at Elegance and the door of Trilok was about 100 feet, so I had to keep a margin of a second.

I suddenly shivered a bit. The mathematics that I had worked out brought to the forefront a gruesome reality. Not only did I have to get my aim perfect, I had to shoot between the 2nd and the 3rd. This meant that my mind had to take aim and shoot extremely quickly. I hadn't trained for that, surprisingly. How the hell had the Major missed the point that I had to almost reflexively get it right? It all seemed to be a whole bloody waste.

Some men kill for pleasure, some for revenge and some kill purely for survival. Right to take a life is best left to God.

Deva, Shree Ganesha

"What do I ask for, Mom?"
"Nothing, son."
"Why, Maa?"
"People who believe they are true
Should stand with folded hands in front of the lord
For no result or desire
But to thank him
He will make you the master of your own luck."

I rushed back to the training site. The Major was standing there. The Major saw a bit of panic in my eyes, "What happened, son? Is the police after you already?"

"No, sir. I do however think I need a year more of training."

Aryan gave me a perplexed look and asked, "Whatever do you mean?"

"Well, no one told me I had one second to release the shot, let alone take aim."

"One second is enough, son. That's almost four times the amount of time you get in the army."

I frowned a bit, "But I'm not an army man. In fact, I'm far from that. I need much more time to aim. Why didn't you time me for that?"

The Major thought for a while and looked at Aryan. "I'll tell you what. Calm down. We'll take you through a round of practice with timed shots. If you think about taking aim for a long time, you end up messing the shot anyway."

I still looked quite panic-stricken, so Aryan tried to calm me down. "Look, come on inside! Let's sit down for a while. We'll then take you to the shooting range."

The Major shook his head in disapproval. "No. He's too focused on his problem right now. If he goes for practice now and by chance misses some shots, it will hit his confidence bad. It will push this mission back by at least a couple of weeks then."

We went in and sat down. The Major asked his help for three cups of tea.

He then took a deep breath and asked, "Any other thing that came to your mind when you were there?"

"I haven't seen Dayashankar personally, you know. I know that you have showed me the photo and I have analyzed his height. I haven't really seen how he moves. I haven't seen who is with him all the time."

I was on a roll, "I haven't even seen what he wears."

Aryan rolled his eyes up a little. "You are not supposed to date him. You are meant to kill him."

"Yeah, yeah. But I need to know more about Pandey."

The Major nodded in agreement. "That can be arranged."

Aryan sighed. "He leads a Ganesha immersion procession for a particular pandal in Dadar. You can be a part of that procession. You have to be careful in terms of how close you get to him. Also, you have to be disguised."

"When is the immersion?"

"In a couple of days."

I then gave Aryan a quizzical look, "How do you know so much about Pandey?"

"I take active interest in the lives of people I am supposed to kill."

"Well, I guess then in a couple of days I get to see the villain of this story."

"Yes."

I was deep in thought when it came to being face to face with the man who murdered Aisha.

Aryan flipped his tongue and said in a villainous tone, "Why so serious?" with a pause on each word.

"You know", smiled Aryan, "Lokmanya Tilak called Lord Ganesha *'The Lord of Everyone'*. Maybe, that's why he allows someone like Pandey to carry him."

"Well, we are going to plot his end there. So, I guess there will be justice by Lord Ganesha."

We all took off from there and even though the Major did not want me to, I took off to the shooting range, albeit without a gun. I stood there for a while and stared at the range. I closed my eyes trying to remember how much time I was exactly taking when I had been aiming for the shot during practice. I just couldn't come to a conclusion and resigned myself to the Major's mansion after some time.

"Ganpati Bappa...."
"Morya, morya."
"Pudhcha baras tu...."
"Laukar yaa."

There were crackers, DJ's blaring microphones, colour being thrown everywhere and just thousands of people on the street. Shouts of Ganpati Bappa Morya were resonating everywhere. People were enjoying themselves to no end. It seemed like such a perfect occasion.

Pandey was leading the procession as part of his PR campaign. He looked reverent in front of the procession which spanned at least five hundred people. For a while there, one could have even mistaken him to be one of the good ones. That is, of course, if you did not know his secret.

In the procession from Dadar led by Pandey, much akin others on the road, people were going absolutely crazy. They were dancing in joy in front of a huge idol of Lord Ganesha who was soon to be immersed in the sea.

There was colour all around and the music was as loud as it could be. Amidst shouts of 'Ganpati Bappa', we made our way forward. It was a small distance, but due to the slow speed of the crowd, my face was full of colour and my clothes were all ragged. With eyes on Pandey, I made my way towards the top of the procession. He was well-guarded by two men who looked to be his permanent bodyguards. Apart from the statue in the vehicle, there was another small idol in Pandey's hands as he made his way to the sea.

I got reasonably close to Pandey. His face had a glow and he was quite hefty. His features were sharp. He was walking slowly. His bodyguards were huge and their faces looked quite blank. My initial judgment was that they seemed quite the type suited more for pushing a crowd or a rowdy man away. They seemed ill-equipped to chase a sniper or determine where a shot came from. But then, I hadn't tested them for that yet.

I looked at him analyzing his moves. I wanted to keep track of everything. Sometimes, people have a tendency to sweat a lot. They tend to get their hands just in front of their heads a lot. That could prove a critical factor in the timing of the shot.

Pandey did not seem to have any idiosyncratic habit that could potentially come in the way of me getting a clear shot of his head. He however tended to keep a little more weight on his left leg than his right while walking. That meant he leant a bit towards the left while walking. If I had to hit the temple, the angle when he went on his left leg would be slightly different from that of his right. That effectively meant I had to let the first step that he took out of the car go just to realize what foot was he on and adjust the shot.

His bodyguards in this case tended to stand about a foot away from their master, both to the left and right. That, I guessed, was probably as close as Pandey wanted to be to them.

My mind was going through many emotions when I was watching him. Aryan and the Major had given me clear instructions not to get emotionally overcome when I saw him. I was supposed to be cold and observe how Pandey walked, his habits, his movement style and anything else that I could.

I kept trying to stress my brain that day, "What should one notice of the man he is about to kill?" It was a difficult question to answer.

He could have been wearing a bulletproof vest. I was, anyway, going to aim at his head. But if I missed and hit his chest or stomach, was a vest protecting him?

There were multiple questions in my head. A preparatory session with him on these questions would have been quite helpful, but I doubt if he would be cooperative in telling me on how to optimize his murder plan.

It would have been great if I could just walk up to him and say, "Pandey, look I want to know a few details about you so that I can plan your murder. I think you need to pay for your deeds and I'm going to help you pay for your bad karma."

We were moving slowly towards the beach. I had my eyes on him the whole time. The beach was quite crowded but his bodyguards ensured that he did not face much difficulty in traversing through the crowd. He was, of course, the privileged one, since he was a public servant.

His bodyguards backed off at the immersion point. Pandey moved in the water alone. He probably wanted some time with God alone. I was about to give him much more time with him soon. Well, technically, neither Pandey nor I were meant for heaven after our death.

Pandey started to move back after the immersion. He moved a tad quicker than his bodyguards and I was standing just on the shore. He walked up and I deliberately stood in his way. He was looking down. We collided and both fell down.

I gave him my hand and said, "Sorry, I didn't see you coming." I accidentally brushed my hand on his chest. The bodyguards quickly moved towards him and he held his hand to keep them back.

My face had a lot of colour on it and was barely recognizable. He looked at me and gave me a dirty look. For that brief moment, Pandey was face to face with the man who was plotting to kill him. Pandey then quickly said "No problem" and walked off.

I don't know if it was in my head or for the few seconds that we were together, Pandey had a premonition about me. I would like to think that there was some fear in his eyes that I sensed. It all felt so surreal.

It was late evening and the sky had an orange tinge on it. As a child, I hated this time of the day. It reminded me of death and gloom. Growing up, I managed to get over this feeling to a degree, yet the feeling of fear remained. Coincidentally, I faced my biggest fear face to face at that time. I had met the man who killed and raped the only woman I ever connected with.

I sat down for a while just to contemplate for a bit. There were a million thoughts going through my head at that time and I just needed to calm myself down a bit.

I went back to the mansion. The Major and Aryan were having a drink. It looked like they were waiting for me to come back.

I sat down next to them casually. Both continued drinking. The Major was smoking what looked like a Cuban Cigar. He was quite the cliché when it came to drinking and smoking.

He offered me a drink and didn't bother to ask me about my experience in the procession. I stayed silent as well, sipping my drink gradually and taking in the fresh air.

Aryan couldn't resist after a while. "So, how was your reconnaissance mission?"

I looked at him and smiled. "It was good. He looked quite menacing, though."

"That's the popular opinion about him. Any other facet of his that you noticed?"

"He walks slightly slower than my assumption when I was calculating the timing of the shot. One of his bodyguards might be someone we have to be wary of. I took a photo of him. Major, you will have to neutralize his movement after the shot."

The Major looked impressed. "You were able to deduce all of that? Have you considered being a mercenary for a living?"

"I did. It's the second best career option for me."

"What's the first?"

"Doing nothing and yet getting a living."

Aryan raised a toast, "Good choice. I assume we are ready for the shot."

I smiled and without the slightest hesitation in my voice help up my glass and said, "Yes. I just have to work a bit more on my timing and we are done."

This was the final phase of my training. I was ready to become a murderer. The unfortunate information that I had gathered from my chance encounter with Pandey was that I had to aim at the head and could not afford to miss that.

I was back at the shooting range in the morning. Aryan was already there. The Major opted out since he believed it to be a non-issue. I took the gun that I was supposed to shoot Pandey with, loaded it and took aim at the circle.

Within minutes, I realized what the Major was saying. If you haven't taken aim in the first one second, you are plain and simple wasting your time. The additional time hardly helped me to improve my shot.

Aryan smiled when he saw me train. He moved towards me and said, "I guess it is time now without any disclaimers."

"Yeah."

"Anything that you are worried about?"

"I don't know what will happen after I kill him."

"We will escape."

"Yeah, I guess I know we will." I then paused for a bit, "You know everything I assumed I knew about myself and my life changed after Aisha. After I lost her, I have been in a state of limbo. I don't know if I have grieved enough, I don't know if I have gotten over that phase, I don't know if killing Pandey will help me sleep well at night. I just know after this that I will have to come to terms with her loss and the fact that things with me and my life will hardly be the same again."

Aryan gave me a pat on the back. "I don't know what to say except that this too shall pass."

I smiled. "I'm sure it will."

He then looked at what I was wearing, "I've never seen you wear this t-shirt. Are you a fan of the man in the print?"

"I wasn't earlier. But, I'm gradually becoming one."

Aryan smiled, "Well, given where you are headed, I'm not surprised."

"Yeah."

I walked off. Not too long ago a man had pointed at the same t-shirt and asked me if I knew who was in that picture.

They say a spark from Lord Ganesha can burn all evil. Yet, leading his procession was Mr. Pandey who was the symbol of all evil. Maybe, I was the man supposed to deliver him to hell and aptly, Ganesha had sent me there to deliver him from his sins. After all, life, creation and the world was all about balance. That was what I had told Aisha at least. I guess I was destined to be the *'Che'* in this story.

People who believe they are true and right should stand with folded hands in front of the divine spirit with no desire of the result. Leave all your fears and stand in front of him. He will make you master of your own luck.

The shot

"How does one focus, Mom?"
"You look at the target, son
Forget everything else
For that moment, nothing else should matter
You need to focus on the eye of the fish,
You will not miss if you do that."

For all the women who have tolerated silently over the years, for all of them who have regarded or disregarded the male form as the advanced race, for all those who have thought of them as the deciders of good or evil and for all of those who have suffered at the hands of miscreants who believe that they can get away with anything, this shot was my gift.

It was targeted at achieving justice when the so-called legal framework failed to deliver in its entirety and left me crippled. This shot was for Aisha's father who saw a child who gave him only love, a man who saw Aisha as a small child barely walking towards her and smiling when coming towards him.

It was pure play vengeance against a man who believed the law was his bitch, who he had domesticated and could manipulate whenever he wanted. Girls were objects whose pain only gave him pleasure. Most importantly, this shot was for me, so I could live and die in peace from here on knowing Mr. Dayashankar Pandey was not going to be alive. It was to end a chapter in my life after which things would take a turn.

The only thing I regretted when I pressed the trigger was that I knew if it hit, the man would die instantly without being able to reflect on why he was suffering this fate. I guess the only justification in my head was when he would pass on to the other side, there would be someone who would explain the reason of his demise to him and make him pay his dues there.

Aryan and Major Singh had just been helping hands who had taken me to this moment. It almost felt at that moment that I was born to take it. This was my purpose, the reason that I was born. Everything else was a side story to the main event.

It turns out that the Major was right. If the pain in your heart reaches the threshold point, your mind focuses on one sole point and you don't miss. Pandey got down from his white Mercedes Benz. Luckily, there was some distance between him and his bodyguards. I got some visual clarity and very little time. He was walking faster than usual. He was probably a metre away from shooting range before I pressed the trigger.

For that split second when it hit him, my eyes went red and Aryan dragged me from there. I saw a little bit of blood on the floor. It had hit him on the temple. We used the rope and went down the building from the reverse side. I went down first. Aryan took out a bottle of petrol and applied the same to the rope while he was slipping on it. We reached the bottom and Aryan lit the rope on fire. It burnt till the top quickly and the remains fell down. We picked the crap that had formed and quickly put it in a bag before rushing out to the main road. The Major was in a car which he had managed to get from his friend for a while.

If I were to create a quick memory of where I committed the most heinous and yet, the most noble moment of my life, I guess I would romanticize the location a tad bit. For a moment, let's forget that it was committed in a marketplace in Mumbai which was by far the most commercial and hence mundane locations around.

I picture it committed with the clouds forming a red looming shadow signifying doom and death. I see a dragon surrounded by this huge fire protecting him from all directions and a mansion just ahead. I see an angel pointing in the direction that I am supposed to point the arrow to. I see an arrow flying off my bow and hitting him straight on the dragon's heart.

All this happened within five minutes. That was exactly the response time it took for the bodyguards to realize what had happened. One of them took a gun out from his pocket and shot it in the air so the place would clear up. It was a bad idea because all he did was create a ruckus. That took them further away from actually figuring out anything about the shot. Turns out they were not very smart.

No shouts, no fear, Mr. Pandey had been hit right on the temple of his head. The sniper in this case deserved an Olympic medal.

I didn't get to see his face. What really happens when one is hit on the head with a bullet? Do the facial expressions change a bit or don't? Every time I saw a photo or reference to Mr. Pandey, there was an arrogant smirk on his face. Was that smirk still there or was I successful in eliminating it? I wanted to make sure he wasn't arrogant in his death. I wanted to know he had that split second of regret before he took off. Maybe people like him probably deserve to die without knowing why.

We burnt the rope as soon as we landed and rushed out of the building via the wall. While we were taking off, I almost heard a noise behind me.

Aryan patted me on my back and said, "Run".

We ran the hell out of the back of the building and realized that there was a man following us. I was sure that he was the bodyguard that I was worried about. He was quite fast and gaining on us.

Aryan pointed me to go into the opposite direction that he was headed. I did not think and followed his instruction immediately.

I was surprisingly faster than Aryan yet the bodyguard seemed more interested to go after me rather than Aryan. I couldn't make out why he was doing that, but I guess that moment was more about instinct than anything else.

The bodyguard clearly had made a wrong choice and my practice helped me considerably. I was able to maintain a safe gap between myself and the guard. He hadn't yet called the police because the moment he stopped to do anything, he knew I was going to be let off.

After about twenty minutes of chasing, we reached the main road. I was deliberately moving towards the Major's pre-decided meeting point. Suddenly, a black Pajero with no number on it started coming between me and the guard. It accelerated towards me.

For a moment, I thought my game was up and the Pajero was after me. It caught up to me and a door opened. Thankfully, I saw Aryan's face and heaved a sigh of relief. I was taken in immediately.

The bodyguard gave up and then started making some calls. The Pajero took a turn down and then vanished from his sight. The Major took the car in a garage and Aryan and me were given separate clothes. He then handed me my ticket to the UK and told me that I had to be at the international airport in an hour's time.

I had a multiple entry visa to UK and they valued me there because I was a high spending tourist. I was more or less a ghost in India and no one knew if I existed. The only card I held was a passport and a bank account number. I did not have a ration card number or anything else. The place my passport was registered to was my parent's residence which had been locked up after their death.

Aryan told me he would get a reliable person to rent out that place for me and never to stay in this country again for more than a month at a stretch. I was more than glad to hear this. He told me funds would be added to my account automatically if I ever fell short. I smiled and took off.

They had my baggage ready in the Jeep they had with them and the Major was to drop me to the airport. We stopped at a store midway.

The Major opened it and kept the weapon in the bag inside the store and parked the jeep there. He then put my baggage in another car and we took off from there. The Major wore his army uniform and carried his ID and other documents with him.

Aryan got a call right there and he looked at the Major. He looked at the Major and said, "I have just been informed my father is dead. I have to go."

I looked at Aryan and asked him sympathetically, "What happened?"

Aryan looked at the Major who nodded his head in approval and then looked at me, "He was shot in the head by someone."

I stared at Aryan in shock. The timing was such that his father had to be Mr. Pandey. The fabric of trust is very tender. It gets ripped off very quickly and you are left naked. It was a split of a second decision for me whether I wanted to confront Aryan or get in the car.

The Major looked at me and said, "Get in the car. I'll explain. You will know Aryan's reason of killing his father before you get out of this country. Right now, we have to act according to plan. You have to trust us."

I got in the car. We drove out. Aryan headed off in the opposite direction.

I looked at the Major. "Will I get some answers now?"

"I know your questions, son. Time you found out about Aryan."

For that moment, nothing else should matter; you need to focus on the eye of the fish, you will not miss if you do that.

The hand that rocks the cradle

"How much did you love your mother, Maa?"
"It matters not how much you love your mother, son
A mother's life revolves around her children,
She loves unconditionally and never expects the same,
They say the hand that rocks the cradle rules the world."

Aryan came to the Major almost in tears.

He looked at the Major, his eyes seething with rage and a deep desire of vengeance. "I want to kill him, sir. I have to kill him."

"Sit down. What happened?"

"I have to kill him, sir. My mother died because of him. I just found out. I want to do it myself."

"He's your father, son."

"Yes, sir but that man-whore got her killed so he could continue his philandering ways."

The Major hugged him while he broke down, "Calm down son. Calm down. How did you find out?"

Aryan calmed down and took a deep breath. "The maid told me she walked in on him forcing himself on another woman. She fought with him over it and told the girl to go away. He slapped her and grabbed the girl with a hand. His loyal bodyguard came in who then held the girl while he pushed my mother away. She hit a wall and bled to death in a corner unattended. He then raped and killed the girl."

He sat himself down and the Major offered him a cup of tea, "Why didn't you kill him as soon as you found out?"

"I am not trained to kill him. I want to do it and get away with it."

He then sighed. "Maybe we can get the legal system to pin him. There's a video recording of the entire incident."

The Major looked up and said, "What?"

"I think he forgot to turn off the CCTV camera at home. He had installed the cameras to make sure no one was stealing from him.

He then looked at the Major with panic and tears in his eyes, "Should I hand this tape over to the police?"

The Major sighed. "The last time he committed a similar crime, there was evidence against him. The case dragged and he somehow managed to buy off and finish off any shred of evidence that could have convicted him. In this case, all he needs to do is finish off this tape before it gets to the Magistrate. Given his contacts in the police, it should be an easy job."

"Maybe, I should give it to the media."

"You could do that and malign his reputation. There is only one problem there, your father has a lot of contacts in that industry. Any such video has a good chance of being traded. Also, even then you are looking at a case which might drag on and the longevity of it will always work in your father's favour."

Aryan was exasperated by then. "So you're telling me I can't do anything."

"He killed your mother, right?"

"Yes, he did."

"You need to get him killed."

Aryan looked at the Major and said, "You mean I should kill him?"

"You are not fit to commit a crime, son. You do not have the perfect vision requisite for such a mission."

"Sir, I am sure I can do it."

"No. I can't train you. There is only one way to kill a politician of your dad's stature. He has to die of a gunshot which has to be perfect. If you miss, the chances of you escaping are miniscule and I doubt whether a man who did not think twice before killing his wife will bother about his son who tried to take his life."

Aryan quietly listened to the Major who he had come to trust over the time that he had known him.

He then silently asked him, "So, let's pay a sharpshooter then."

He sighed. "This can't be a paid mission. Most of these sharpshooters have illicit connections which link back to politicos like your dad. These connections pose a real risk in soliciting any such assignment through them. Also, these guys can be tracked post the incident which in itself is a risk."

"I should just let him be."

The Major took out a cigar and lit it up. "You know, in the mythological era, the principles of natural justice were said to be operational in this world. Ravana faced his end because he kidnapped Sita. Duryodhana was punished for trying to unclothe Draupadi. He had to face an all-out war with the Pandavas. Good won over evil. It was the time of the gods."

Aryan was slightly irritated because he felt the Major had just diverted and probably trivialized the issue, but he didn't want to express it so he played along, "Isn't our law also based on the principles of natural justice?"

"I guess the difference between then and now is just greed. You can buy the arbitrators, and the perpetrators of injustice generally go scot-free. The amount of time you spend in jail is inversely proportional to the money that a criminal is willing to spend."

"Yeah. This is *'Kalyug'* as opposed to *'Satyug'* back then." He had lost his patience by then. "Sir, I'm sorry but I just figured out my father murdered my mother. Do you have anything that is relevant for me?"

"Well, yes and no. I believe that you may not directly have the capacity to avenge your mother, but you have the drive to develop another."

"Who?"

"You have to find someone who has been wronged by your father. It should not be difficult given that he has committed so many crimes. He must have harmed many women. You need to try and find out if any of them have a boyfriend, husband or brother who is craving for justice."

"Why do you think these boyfriends, husbands or brothers have been silent so far?"

"Well, I'm sure a lot of them are trying to figure out who did this to the girl they loved. Your father must have done a great job in destroying evidence."

"You want me to go and tell them I know who killed your girl. They will probably think I did it. To top it up, I should probably add the little fact that my father did it. They will then help me kill him. Do you see the irony of the situation? Most of them would want to get me murdered."

"You would want to leave that part off and you have to reveal to the family of the girl in a sinister way so that they don't start the legal process."

"Which my father will quash?"

"Yes, you need to search for a rebel from the affected who failed the legal route, which they were bound to."

"Right."

"I will help train the man. We will make him the perfect weapon trained to kill."

Aryan went silent for a while, "How do I find the evidence if it was destroyed?"

"I'm sure your father had a high degree of complacency in not destroying all evidence when you know it's within your control. You may have the luxury to access it. In fact, you already have a tape."

"Right."

"Let's try and start with that then. Try and see who that girl was."

Aryan nodded his head. Frustration was written all over his face. He just wanted instant revenge. He clenched his fists and blurted out, "I just wish someone gave me a gun so I could have my vengeance. I don't understand why my mother thought it was her religion to continue living with that bastard. I just don't understand why she didn't leave him. The worst part is, even if she did, he wouldn't have cared."

He then kept his tea on the table and sighed. "Indian women of that generation were very difficult to understand. Even if their husbands were the scum of the earth, they would do everything for him. She took care of him while he abused her mentally and physically. She would make tea for him while he lusted about his next target in his head. That man deserves to be hung by his genitals."

The Major was silent while Aryan was talking. There were tears in his eyes. He got up and got a bottle of Jack Daniels with some soda.

He then looked at him and smiled, "I should have got this before."

Aryan gave a defeated smile and took a glass from him. "Like all mothers, she was the only one who believed I could never go wrong, you know. I kept on telling her to leave that bastard and that god damn house but she didn't. She just wouldn't listen to me."

He sipped down his glass as fast as he could. The Major gave him a refill and then kept his hand on Aryan's shoulder, "Manage your thirst well, son. Don't be in a hurry."

"For the drink or for his bloody heart?"

"Both."

The drinks kept on going down with intermittent flashes of Aryan reminiscing memories of his dead mother.

All of a sudden on his fourth or fifth drink, he said, "He raped the girl in our house."

"Yeah. So?"

"He didn't even bother to think about the CCTV that he's installed in the house. I have to find out more about that girl."

"I think he believes he's far above the law. It's actually true. He's a politico and their kind controls almost everything there is to control in this country. How old did the girl look?"

"I think this girl was young. She must have been around twenty-five."

"Do you know anything about her?"

"The maid mentioned her name, I think."

"How did she know? That would be a great starting point."

"I think Pandey knew her name. He probably found out from somewhere before he did his dirty act on her."

"So who was it?"

"I think she said Aisha."

She loves unconditionally and never expects her children to do the same. They say the hand that rocks the cradle rules the world

Satyamev Jayate

"Does the truth always win, Maa?"
"Life has varied realities, son
Different versions of the truth
It is not up to us humans to judge and decide the truth
Easier to believe that what happened is right
And part of a larger truth that we don't know."

I had just killed someone and was at peace with myself. Somehow, the desire to go back to my life just wasn't there. I had to go to London for a while so that there was no trace of me. I was a ghost as usual with limited proof of existence. My passport was managed well by Aryan. It was no surprise, given his political contacts.

I hoped there was no redemption for Pandey up there. I had given him a swift death so the Karmic cycle was not really complete. Someone had to screw up with his soul up there to even things out for me.

Mr. Dayashankar Pandey's death sparked an outrage. Aryan was supposed to light fire to his pyre which he did. He cried in front of everyone else and politicians expressed their condolences to him. They vowed to avenge his death and bring the murderer to justice. Most blamed his murder on the opposition and said people will avenge Dayashankar's death by giving a clear mandate against the opposition.

Aryan reiterated their statements and said that people will make the opposition party pay for his father's death and that his father taught him to serve the people with all he had and he would carry his father's honorable legacy into the future. It was just amazing how you could outright lie to the public in politics. Media was rife at Pandey's funeral. Breaking news that day was how Aryan would carry his father's legacy. I wonder what would have happened had they found out Aryan planned his murder. It would have been breaking news for a month.

Except for Aryan and other politicos, not many relatives came to the funeral. No one cared much for him. Many a times, we think these powerful men can get what they want and that the world gives a shit. The truth is people tolerate their crap because they have to and the man isn't missed much.

When everyone left and no one was around, Aryan spat on Mr. Pandey's pyre and prayed for the redemption of his mother's soul.

He collected his ashes the next day like a dutiful son. He went home and replaced the ashes with some sand in another pot. He immersed them in the Ganges with local media present. He threw Pandey's ashes in the gutter.

The police interrogated Aryan to find out who may have killed Mr. Pandey. Aryan pointed fingers at a few politicians who had always wanted to take his father's place. Aryan was informed by his father's party that he would be given a ticket to stand for the upcoming assembly elections given that the public sympathy factor was with him. He gladly took up the offer and went with the flow.

No one wanted a conclusion to Mr. Pandey's case. There was not going to be any vengeance for his soul. There weren't even any meaningful tears shed there.

London became my home. It was good to be in a country where the law worked and no one spat on the road at random while blaming the system for the dirt around. It got me thinking as to what worked in India and what did not. Lack of systems in the country exposed what India had truly become. If you had money and power, you could have your way. If you didn't have money, you might still get away with anything because of the nonchalance. The only way the systems in the country trapped you was if you pissed off a man richer and/or more powerful than you.

India was even more horrifying a place for me to visit after Aisha's death than it had been after my mother's. That coupled with the fact that I had absolutely no one to go back to ensured I wasn't going back there for as long as I could.

I was stationed at Sommerset Bayswaters just near Notting Hill and Aryan had ensured that along with my father's savings, I did not have to work all my life and could continue living a wasted life like I had before.

London is a wonderful city, especially if you have nothing to do there. The people are nice, the bars are awesome and the girls are approachable. There is a slight degree of arrogance in the Brits but they have ruled most of the world for the better half of the eighteenth and the nineteenth century and have probably inherited that arrogance.

I had to just take a walk down the lane and groceries were aplenty. Tesco and Tesco junior were everywhere. The area had a colonial feel to it, much akin a few places in South Bombay which still reflects the British architecture to a degree.

I liked walking down the streets in the evening, drowning myself in drinks in the night and getting up at leisure in the morning. I deserved a break, given that I had just cleaned out some scum in India.

Four months later, I was walking down the lane when a hand tapped me on the back. I turned to see Major Singh and Aryan smiling at me.

Aryan started the conversation, "You've had coffee?"

"Not really."

"Let's go grab a cup then."

We took off to the nearest café and took a seat. It was a typical English café with teak wood tables and archaic English chairs.

"So, how's life been?"

"Okay, I guess. I wasn't expecting to see you again like ever."

Aryan smiled, "You will meet us at various points in your life. I might want a lot of other people murdered, you know. I'm joining politics and it can be quite a dirty profession."

"You'll be much better in it than your Dad was."

"You're too kind."

I looked at Aryan with the expectation that he would tell me more. I wanted to know the complete story of the murder.

Aryan realized there were some questions still to be answered, "You need closure on this, don't you?"

"I guess I do."

"My full name as you already know is Aryan Dayashankar Pandey. I am told the Major told you about my mother already."

"Yes, he did."

"I was the one who sent you the video. I was supposed to find out about Aisha. I couldn't figure out anyone related to her who would be capable for the murder. When I asked a few people, someone apparently had seen you enter her room and believed you had some sort of a connection with her. I got all your details via my sources. It took me some time. You are almost a ghost. Actually, the fact that tracing you was so difficult made me even more confident that you were the man for this job. I then planted a copy of the tape in your room and voila."

"Why did you let Bhim get convicted?"

"I couldn't stop what was going on. The tape has a minor glimpse of Aisha that I knew people close to her would recognize. There weren't many people close to her. It was not very good evidence. Given my dad's deep pockets, it was almost a waste. I had nothing. Also, my dad had pushed for Bhim's conviction. He put forth a good prosecution and the judge was paid for. There was enough public outrage to convict anyway. Also, I wanted my father dead for what he did. Given how he manipulated the law, it was impossible to get him convicted or punished for anything in India."

"Why didn't you tell me about your relationship with him?"

"You would never have trusted me."

"I could have."

"I didn't want to take a chance."

"What are the risks of me ever getting caught?"

"None."

"Why?"

"The real killer of Mr. Pandey has been apparently identified. He was killed by a rival politician, Mr. Iyer who is trapped in the case. Mr. Iyer went to no length to convince me he did not do it and paid me off to divert the police. We then implicated a man who was killed by the police in an encounter. They needed a strong case against him and we gave them this. Technically, in the entire fiasco, Mr. Iyer is the killer who got away and I am the man who accepted a bribe to let him."

"So you got your father killed, got his money and got money for saving someone who wasn't involved in the entire fiasco?"

"Yes." He smiled and continued, "I also got an assembly seat. The by poll elections were held immediately and I won because of public sympathy."

"You're definitely a politico."

"Yes. I did make sure that we convicted a hard core criminal though. He wasn't guilty of this crime but of many others. How are you doing?"

"I'm okay. Still not fully over Aisha yet, I guess."

Aryan sighed, "Were you guys in a very committed relationship?"

"If you had any doubts of, how did you trust my motive?"

"The feeling of almost being in love with playboys like you tends to be stronger than actual love. You wouldn't have been able to sustain that feeling once the mystery died out. The fact that she was still a partial mystery to you helped."

"You judge my emotions. This is after you used them to make me execute someone in cold blood. I was very much in love."

"Yeah. And how do you feel about it?"

"Not bad, actually. Keep me away from those bars and I'm happy about it."

"Done. How's London?"

"Not bad. I have never been in a place for so long. That is, except the Major's place of course, and since we were on a mission, it didn't seem that long there."

It was a nice, long session after days. As the sun descended, our spirits did not and we continued through the night going to whatever place would take us in. It was strange. At that moment, there were only two people who were probably aware that I existed. Before I met them and in the time that Aisha had died, there was none. I see people talk ill of their friends and family, but it must be good for them to at least know that their life matters, their existence makes sense.

That evening, the Major decided to call it in early and Aryan and I headed to a bar.

We ordered a couple of drinks and he raised his glasses, "Cheers."

I responded back and he gave me a piercing look, "So, have you met anyone here?"

"No one."

"How come?"

"I guess I'm not looking."

"You need to get over her."

I guzzled down the beer and asked for another one and then looked at him, "You know, in the case of Aisha, the mystery was actually over and I had feelings for her beyond that. I don't know how much of myself I could have bared beyond all that I had shared with her. She knew everything there was to know about me. The funny thing was that even after that, I hardly saw a judgmental look."

"Hey, I'm sorry when I said playboys like you only last till the mystery does."

"No, no. What you said was true. I just don't know how Aisha worked out differently."

There were a few tears in my eyes and the beer kept flowing. After about three/four drinks, I just remember saying Aisha's name out loud a lot of times. In fact, the bartender came and asked Aryan if his name was Aisha and why was he making me sad.

The evening passed away quickly that day. We were all quite out of our senses that day. The night gave way to the next day. In the morning, they were supposed to go back and resume their lives. Life was to go on for them. I hoped they would remember me, if only as the assassin. At least then I would have someone from my past still alive.

The Major told Aryan he wanted to talk to me before leaving on early morning coffee.

I sat in a chair, curious to hear what he had to say to me. My mentor, trainer, torturer was about to say a few words.

"Son, you okay?"

"Yes."

"You do know you loved her, right?"

"I did not. Didn't you hear Aryan say I was almost in love? I'm a playboy."

"How many girls have you slept with while you were here?"

"None."

"Do you still think about her?"

"No."

"Don't lie to me."

"Well, sometimes."

"Well, Aryan's a kid. I'm not. You were hurting when you came to me and had enough motive to commit a murder without any fear of the consequences. You learnt fast and killed clean. You were in love with her and what he did pained you in your guts. In fact, that pain made you the perfect weapon."

"It was about justice."

"How many girls are getting raped in India, son? I don't see you seeking justice and balance there."

"No."

He then held me by my shoulders, "You need to go to a support group. There are families of rape victims who meet up in London. You should go there and talk about your loss. Once you feel it, you will be able to let go. Trust me, son. I've been there."

"Your wife was raped."

"No, a girl I loved, who married someone else was killed by a rapist."

I stared at him for a while, a few tears in my eyes and said, "I'll think about it."

He put his hands on my shoulders and was about to leave.

I stopped him, "He said you knew stories from his childhood. You now are saying your love was killed by a rapist. I have trained under you. I know you cannot be caught…not by a rookie like Aryan. You exposed yourself to him and got him under your wing."

The Major smiled.

"The woman you loved was Aryan's mother, I said."

The Major looked at me and kept a hand on his heart. With his characteristic style, he said, "From the bottom of my heart, son."

"Is Aryan your son? Did you make him use me because you didn't want him involved?"

He just smiled. "Don't be silly. That's stretching it."

Aryan shouted from outside, "Major, are you ready?"

I stopped the Major, "I want my answers."

"Some questions, son, are best left to the imagination and their answers can lead to no good."

That bullshit was the last thing the Major told me before he left; cursing me to a lifetime of conundrum and no clear answers to a lot of questions.

Easier to believe that what happened is right. And part of a larger truth that we don't know.

I Want To Live

"What is it that keeps us going even after all difficulties, Maa?"
"The instinct for survival keeps us going
The desire to live and continue
You are alive until you have the desire to live, son
You are alive until you want to live."

You don't realize it when it happens. You try and block it out after it has happened, but it has to hit some time if you haven't gotten over it. It hurts like hell once you realize it.

It hit me when I started to acknowledge the fact that Aisha was the only one I ever really felt something for. She was no longer there and some desperate ass had taken her away from me. I had prevented myself from imagining any part of the pain that Aisha may have suffered in that gruesome incident. It is difficult if you picture a living soul who you were close to and who was tortured. The images don't make sense. They just don't.

There was one support group where you could go and express how you felt. It was for relatives of people who had lost their loved ones to rape and sexual violence. People also apparently talked about rape and the root causes, how to eliminate them and what needs to be done to get rid of this menace.

Does the technical definition of rape suffice to manifest what the crime is? Rape is much beyond everything that's ever written in law books. It is a much worse crime than described in Section 375 of the Indian Penal Code. Most crimes are a moment of madness generally brought about by rage or greed. Lust is probably the worst of sins.

It was a small room with eight to ten people who had got together to mourn their loved ones who were victims of rape. One of them lost her seven-year-old girl to an old, desperate, sick man. One had lost her eighteen-year-old daughter. There were all kinds of horror stories there.

Everyone had already recounted their stories and this was an opportunity to express and be able to carry on with some sort of a normal existence. I guess apart from the one who has left, the rapist manages to torture and kill even the ones left behind for a good amount of time.

"My child came to me in my sleep last night and was constantly asking for a new doll and I just kept on telling her no. I don't know why I didn't get the world for her. She was my only daughter. I should have let her have that doll. She kept on insisting, then she started to cry, and before I knew it they turned into shouts, shrieks of pain. I couldn't take it. I can't take it. These dreams haunt me every night and every living moment of my life."

"I always imagined my child would go on to have a great job and meet her prince charming and be happy. That old, menacing bastard stole her away and we found her body without any clothes in a dump a few days later."

"My wife was very beautiful. She worked late nights. I kept on telling her not to work very late. We used to fight and she never listened. I loved her so much. It's become impossible for me to have any relationship with anyone after her. She's taken a part of me with her."

"You see, we each want to individually torture the men who did this to our loved ones, but that is not the solution. The solution is that there has to be a change in the mindset of people right from the early years. Boys need to be taught to respect women."

"That means you are looking at changes in the next generation."

"Yeah. Any movement that we start or try to propagate will benefit the next generation. One generation suffers, the second rebels and the third benefits."

I spoke up, "That is a long term solution. What happens to the girls who suffer now? What happens to the women who deserved to live, to work, to have dreams, to meet someone who loves them. They deserved to live on."

"You go on and on about there being balance, Dhruv. You are quite disconnected with the world, aren't you?"

"It's my world view, Aisha. It is quite consistent with the Karma theory."

"Hmm… You also have a theory about falling in love, do you?"

"I didn't have any theory up until now. I'm starting to develop one now."

"I have my own theory about love."

"Please state it for my enlightenment."

"When one person is ready to put the other person's life and interests above his own, the said first person is in love."

"So, I have to put my life on the line to prove my love to you."

She smiled, "That depends."

"On what?"

"That depends on whether you really are in love with me."

I was asked to narrate what happened to Aisha. I could hardly speak. I was in tears and had lost absolute control of myself. I would talk about how a powerful person kidnapped and raped Aisha. How he ravaged her so much that she could hardly speak after the incident.

Some people started to move towards me to calm me down and the moderator stopped them, "He needs to grieve. Somehow, I don't think he's grieved for her yet. Let him cry."

I cried for a long time, managing a sentence or two about the incident in gaps. The moderator kept the group's focus on me and people around me also had tears in their eyes.

I was almost done talking about the incident and was out of tears.

The moderator asked me what was the one thing that reminded me again and again about the incident?

I just said, "While she was in the hospital fighting for her life, she looked at me and asked for a piece of paper and a pen. I thought she wanted to tell me who did this to her so I could fight for her. I thought she wanted to tell me to take revenge and make that guy pay…but she didn't write that. On that piece of paper, she wrote something that will haunt me for the rest of my life."

The group stared at me, tears in all of their eyes as well. One or two even held me close and tried to calm me down.

I took out the piece of paper from my pocket and put it down in front of absolute strangers who had but just one thing in common.

The paper said, 'Dhruv, I want to live….'

You are alive until you have the desire to live, son. You are alive until you want to live.